The One Who Tells the Stories

The One Who Tells the Stories

A Boy, a Girl, One Week, & God

James A. Tweedie

Dunecrest Press

Table of Contents

Chapter One
Fil and the Elijah Boys
Sunday Afternoon & Evening

"But I don't want to go to camp!"

Twelve-year old LaShaun Delanton was about to spend a week at middle school church summer camp. He was not a happy camper. He didn't want to be there; he didn't know anyone and even after his father had registered him at the camp office he was still begging to go home.

LaShaun's father put a hand on his shoulder.

"Remember, the Bible says, 'Trust in the Lord with all your heart and do not lean on your own understanding . . .'"

LaShaun cut him off.

"Yeah, I know, '. . . in all your ways acknowledge him and he will make your paths straight.'"

"LaShaun," his father whispered, "if you trust him, God will give you a great week at camp."

"Sure," LaShaun muttered, "and if God likes camp so much maybe you should have signed up Jesus to go instead of me!"

He picked up his backpack and sleeping bag and walked over to a large granite boulder. He felt like crying but instead he bit his tongue . . . until it hurt.

When he turned around, his father was gone.

LaShaun had been assigned to Cabin #7, a small, rustic, wooden building with five bunk beds inside and the name "Elijah" posted over the door. From Sunday school he knew that Elijah was an Old Testament prophet who had been carried up to heaven in a fiery chariot. As LaShaun stowed his gear on the lower half of a bed, he decided the inside of the cabin must have been as hot as Elijah's chariot. It was mid-July, the outside afternoon air was a blazing 92 degrees, and the stale air of the uninsulated cabin felt like an oven. Now he was sure he was not going to enjoy his week at Gold Creek Bible Camp.

The camp, located in the high foothills of California's Sierra Nevada Mountains, covered an area where Gold Creek emptied into Lake El Dorado. Although the camp was just a thirty-minute drive east of Grass Valley, it had taken over three hours to get there from LaShaun's home in Marin County. He was considering the possibility of hitchhiking home when the camp bell rang, signaling it was time for everyone to gather at the campfire circle.

At the campfire circle, he noticed some of the kids were sitting in groups as if they might have been from the same church. Others were sitting as far from everyone else as they could. LaShaun found a place on a section of a bench that was empty because it was in the full heat of the sun.

He was wearing shorts and when his bare legs touched the hot bench it felt like the time he had tipped over his mother's morning cup of coffee onto his pants. He had only been six years old when it happened, but he had never liked the smell of coffee since. He had even made a vow to God that he would never touch the stuff when he got old enough to drink it.

The camp director was a man with a smile that looked as though it would disappear as soon as he walked back into his office. The smile was accompanied by a laugh that sounded about the same as the smile looked. LaShaun thought the man looked a little older than his father and the thought of his father made him start to feel sad and lonely again.

The Director gave a long speech that could have been shortened to the single word, "Hello." The Director then introduced a girl who looked as if she had just graduated from high school. Her name was Worthy.

She cut to the chase and just said, "Hi."

LaShaun decided right away that she seemed nice enough and hoped he could be in her group. Worthy explained she was the head camp counselor and that it was her job to introduce the kids to their cabin counselors.

The counselor for LaShaun's cabin was a twenty-year-old boy with acne named "Fil-with-an-F." Fil was thin and scrawny. His brown hair looked as though it had never been introduced to a comb and his wire-rimmed glasses had lenses that looked as if they were thick enough to start a fire if the sun was focused through them onto a pile of dry leaves.

Fil somehow managed to garble the only words he said, "I'm good . . . uh . . . I mean I'm glad to be here and . . . uh . . . a counselor and . . . uh . . . yeah . . . a counselor . . . uh . . . Hi!."

He looked and sounded like an idiot. But since LaShaun sometimes felt the same way about himself he decided to cut Fil some slack and see what sort of counselor he was before writing him off as a waste of time.

Worthy asked all of the Elijah boys to raise their hands and had them form a group off to the side around Fil. There were eight boys assigned to

4

LaShaun's cabin, and he wondered why there weren't ten to fill up all the beds.

The boys were a mixed bag. Some seemed a lot older than LaShaun and looked like they played football and lifted weights. A few were smaller than he was and there was one Asian-looking kid and one kid who was black like LaShaun's father. It was a group he figured might just turn out to be okay.

Fil said that because they were boys he wasn't going to ask them to hold hands but he did ask them to close their eyes and bow their heads while he gave a little prayer. The prayer sounded as if Fil had written it out and then tried to memorize it. The prayer went like this:

"Heavenly Father, I hope this will be a fun week for all of us and that everyone will get to know Jesus better and . . . ."

Fil stopped as if he could not remember what was supposed to come next.

" . . . and . . . " he tried again,

" . . . and that it will be a fun week for all of us. Amen."

When LaShaun opened his eyes, he saw that Fil didn't look at all embarrassed for messing up his prayer; embarrassed like LaShaun would have felt if he had done something as stupid as that. To his surprise Fil was just standing there, smiling as if messing up was something he did so often he had stopped worrying about it.

Fil had everyone sit, say their name, and tell something interesting about themselves. Colin, one of the younger-looking boys went first.

"I just came back from a two-week trip to Europe with my parents. I liked Paris best."

Another boy, named "Phil-with-a-'Ph,'" said he could play the piano.

Robert, who was one of the older boys, said his father was the church pastor and could read Greek.

"That is interesting, Robert." Fil said. "But could you tell us something about yourself instead of about your father?"

Robert said he couldn't think of anything at the moment, but he would let them know if he thought of something.

When it was LaShaun's turn to say his name, two of the boys raised their hands at the same time and asked, "How do you spell that?"

They looked at each other and started to laugh as though it was funny.

LaShaun didn't think it was funny at all and wished he were back home spending the summer watching TV or playing on the computer.

"Be nice, boys," Fil interrupted, "and let LaShaun finish sharing about himself."

LaShaun didn't want to share anything at all, but because everyone was sitting around waiting for him to talk, he felt pressured to say something, so he did.

"Before school let out for the summer, I ran all the way around the football field during P.E. without stopping which was a really big deal because I have asthma."

As soon as he said it, he wished that he hadn't. To the other boys it probably sounded like a really dumb thing to say.

Fil said, "All right LaShaun! That's fantastic! I have asthma, too, and I know how big a deal that is. Let's all give LaShaun a big hand!"

The other boys looked around at each other not knowing what to do. None of them could figure out why they should clap for something like that but Fil was standing up, clapping his hands and saying, "Woo-hoo, LaShaun!"

Some of them clapped, some of them didn't and LaShaun didn't know whether to feel good or bad about the whole thing. He felt bad about the other boys being forced to clap but he felt good about Fil standing up for him and sharing that he had asthma, too.

After the introductions were over, Fil led them to two picnic tables where they made nametags and learned how to braid long, narrow pieces of flat plastic into the shape of crosses they could wear around their necks for the rest of the week. LaShaun's cross turned out lopsided and the arms of the cross were two different sizes, but some of the other boys didn't even finish theirs before Fil led them to the cabin and showed them where they could wash up for dinner.

At dinner, LaShaun sat next to the black kid who was from Berkeley. His name was Mo.

"I don't have a dad," Mo said matter-of-factly as he chewed on a carrot stick. "My Mom's a nurse's aide at Alta Bates Hospital and I've got an older brother and a younger sister. My grandpa was coach for the Berkeley High School baseball and basketball teams but then he died."

Mo talked a lot which was fine with LaShaun, who didn't feel like sharing details about his own family with anyone.

After dinner, the camp kids had some free time to explore the camp. LaShaun walked around by himself and when the bell rang, he joined everyone else at the campfire circle.

As the sun set, a cool breeze swept down from the mountains and whispered through the trees. The campfire danced and crackled; popping burning embers into the air like shooting stars. Wood smoke blew everywhere and most of the kids tried to keep as far away from it as possible.

Worthy turned out to be the worship leader. She played guitar and sang all the songs LaShaun knew from church; the same ones LaShaun's father listened to when he cooked dinner.

Until the worship and singing began, everything at camp had seemed strange and foreign to LaShaun. That all changed when the singing started. When he sang, he felt he had finally found something that reminded him of home and, for the first time all day, he felt good about being at camp.

One of the counselors read a verse from the Bible and gave a short devotion about someone whose name sounded something like "Mefiboseth;" a name LaShaun had never heard of before. The devotion was all about being different from everyone else but that it didn't really matter because God loves everyone anyway, no matter who they are.

LaShaun felt as though the story was about himself, but he already knew that God loved him and that his family did, too—at least most of them. The thought of love led him to wonder if there would ever be a girl who would love him enough to marry him. Thinking about that made him feel uncomfortable so he was relieved when Worthy ended the campfire with a prayer.

Before everyone went back to their cabins, the counselors brought out coat hangers, graham crackers, chocolate bars and marshmallows to make s'mores.

There were lots of kids but the campfire was big enough for them to hold their marshmallows over the dying coals and roast them the way they liked them best. When marshmallows caught on fire, some of the kids tried to blow them out, but others waved them over their heads and ran around as if they were torches.

LaShaun had never made s'mores before. He took a long time to carefully roast his marshmallow light brown on each side before he mushed it between the chocolate and graham crackers. It tasted so good that he made a second one.

By the time everyone had finished, the fire had burned down to a soft glow and there were sticky fingers and lips everywhere. Some kids had melted marshmallow in their hair, on their clothes and even on the bottom of their shoes. Everyone, including LaShaun, had a good time.

After Worthy collected all the hangers, she sent everyone back to their cabins for the night.

When LaShaun got back to the Elijah cabin he found that the temperature inside was about the same as the inside of his bedroom at home. Later he found that it got a lot colder between then and the next morning.

After brushing their teeth, the boys changed their clothes into pajamas or t-shirts and boxers. LaShaun changed his clothes inside his sleeping bag. Some of the other boys did this too, but the football-type boys seemed comfortable changing out in front of everybody. He wondered if he would ever feel comfortable enough to do that but after a moment or two, he decided probably not.

When they were in bed Fil gave each of them a small notebook along with a pencil and said they were supposed to write stuff in it every night before "lights out."

Mo asked, "What are we supposed to write about?"

"Anything you want. But if you saw God somewhere during the day you should write that down, too."

LaShaun had never thought about seeing God somewhere and he couldn't figure out what Fil meant by it. So, he left out the part about God and wrote down how bad he felt when his father drove away and how Worthy and Fil were nice and how he had met Mo. He started to tell what he had for dinner but decided it wasn't important enough to write down. He did, however, write down the word "Mefiboseth" so he could look for it in his Bible or ask his father about it when he got home.

After a few minutes Fil said, "That's it. Stop writing. If you didn't finish you can do the rest of it tomorrow. It's time for lights-out in ten seconds: Ten, nine, eight . . ."

When he got to zero, he flipped the light switch by the cabin door next to his bunk and the room went dark.

LaShaun noticed that Fil didn't share his bunk with anyone else. Now he understood why there were ten beds and only eight boys. LaShaun figured that Fil slept next to the door to keep track of anyone who tried to sneak out or who had to go to the bathroom during the night.

He was just about to close his eyes when someone in the bunk next to him said, "Hey, Fil, tell us a story."

Some of the boys groaned but another voice said, "Yeah, tell us a story. A real good one. You know, a scary one!"

The groans lost the vote as other boys started to chant, "We want a story! We want a story! We want a story!"

Somewhere in the darkness Fil said, "Quiet! Knock it off or Worthy will come over to see if someone's killing a fatted calf or something."

There was a short pause, and LaShaun thought he heard a soft sigh.

"Okay," Fil said. "If you'll all be quiet, I'll tell you a story. But if anyone interrupts me or starts making noise I'll stop. Got it?"

LaShaun and the other boys wanted to say, "Yes, we got it!" but they were afraid if they said it out loud, they would be making a noise and then Fil wouldn't tell his story; so, none of them said anything at all.

After another short pause, Fil said, "Well? What's with you guys? Do you want me to tell you a story or not?"

LaShaun couldn't keep his mouth from saying, "Yes, please, tell us a story."

The boys lay in their beds, quiet and still in the dark cabin. The sound of Fil clearing his throat broke the silence, and the story began.

"Gold Creek Camp is not too far from Interstate 80, the highway that goes up into the High Sierra and crosses Donner Pass. That reminds me of another story I could tell you some time . . . but not tonight. Just past Donner Lake you can turn right and drive up the Truckee River to an even bigger lake called Lake Tahoe. I bet most of you have heard of Lake Tahoe and that some of you have actually been there. The lake is almost two thousand feet deep and the water is very, very cold, and the deeper you go the colder it gets.

"Anyway, there are some really big fish in Lake Tahoe. The biggest kind is called a Mackinaw Trout. Some people call it a Lake Trout but as far as this story is concerned it doesn't really matter. These big fish like to swim along the bottom of the lake, especially where the deep water starts to get shallower; where the deep blue water starts to turn a lighter blue and then green. People who fish for them run their boats slowly along those places while they let out several hundred feet of heavy fishing line, usually with a wooden lure called a plug at the end of it.

"To catch one of these big fish you have to keep the plug as close to the bottom as possible, but there's a lot of moss down there and dead trees with branches and stuff you can catch your hook on. When I was little, I used to go out with my dad just before sunrise. We usually spent half the time trying to get his plug off one of those underwater trees. You really have to know your stuff if you are going to catch one of those fish."

A falling pinecone clunked on the cabin roof and interrupted the story. It chattered as it rolled down and over the side, making a softer "clunk" when it hit the ground. When the distraction was over, Fil picked up where he had left off.

"My dad used to fish in a place he called "The Hole." It was a short stretch of water at the south end of the lake. My grandfather had fished there when he was a young man and there were still a few old-timers left who fished there, too. One of them was a man named Harry Baines. One day when we were over at Harry's cabin, he told us a story."

Someone sneezed and Fil paused for a moment until the room was quite again.

"Before I tell you the rest, I've got to tell you that Harry liked to go out on the lake a lot earlier than anyone else. He liked it best when it was still dark, before the sun came up. When we went out just before sunrise, we often saw Harry's boat already heading back to shore.

"Harry told us how one morning, when it was so dark he could hardly see the water, his plug hit something that didn't seem to move. At first, like most fishermen he thought it might be a fish, a really big fish. But it didn't take him long to figure out that he had hooked a dead tree or a large branch. He turned the boat in every direction hoping he could pull the plug free but, after a long while, he decided he was going to have to pull hard enough to break the plug off the line, reel everything in, and start all over. He stopped the engine on his boat and pulled as hard as he could. Instead of snapping the line where the plug was tied, whatever it was at the bottom of the lake moved a little and then came up off the lake bottom with the plug still attached.

"For a fisherman on Lake Tahoe this is absolutely the worst thing that can happen. Because now, to get it off, you have to reel the line all the way up to the surface. Harry had hooked something very heavy and he muttered to himself and maybe even said a few bad words while he slowly and painfully reeled in the three hundred feet of copper line.

"When the sun is up the water in Lake Tahoe is so clear that you can see down a long way, but Harry was fishing before the sun was all the way up and he couldn't see much of anything. When he had only 25-feet of line left he felt one last tug and the heavy weight disappeared. The hooks on his plug had come free. He knew that the plug could have snapped off, the hooks could have bent, or have moss caught on them, so he reeled in the last bit of line to check it out.

"When he got the line all the way up, he pulled it out of the water and into his boat. The first light of the sun was just beginning to peek over the mountains to the east and in that dim, early morning light, he saw that something was still hooked onto his plug. It was a shoe."

Fil stopped talking. There was silence. LaShaun couldn't even hear the sound of anyone breathing, including himself. All he could think about was that shoe.

After a few moments Fil said, "Good-night boys." And that was the end of it.

As the boys settled into their sleeping bags, the creaking of bedsprings and the smell of old plastic mattresses hushed them to sleep like a lullaby.

Chapter Two
Marcy
Monday Morning

The next morning Fil made sure everybody in the cabin was awake in time for Day-Start Devotions. To begin, he asked Glen, one of the older boys, to read a verse from the Bible.

When Glen had finished Fil said, "I want each of you to tell me what you think this verse is saying to you."

After the sharing was over, Fil handed Mo an index card with a prayer written on it and asked him to read it aloud.

Devotions were over but before everyone left for breakfast, Fil had one last thing he wanted to say.

"Uh, boys, I mean, guys . . . About last night and the story thing . . . the one I told you . . . maybe it would be a good idea if you . . . if . . . you know . . . you don't tell anyone about it? You see, I was thinking and I don't think Worthy or the director or some of your parents would think it was a good story to tell you at Bible Camp. I don't know why. But that's what I was thinking about afterward. I mean . . . I'm okay with it and . . . well, you know . . . Okay? . . . Okay . . . let's get some breakfast."

LaShaun didn't see why any of it had to be such a big secret but Fil's little talk had made the story seem more interesting than ever. For LaShaun, the Elijah cabin had become even more special now that they knew something no one else did.

But LaShaun also noticed that when Fil talked about stuff, he didn't say it very well but when he told the story about Lake Tahoe and the shoe, he had told it perfectly without sounding clumsy or stupid at all.

While they were eating pancakes in the dining hall Mo asked LaShaun what the story was supposed to have been about.

"I didn't get it," Mo said. "So, a guy goes fishing and catches a shoe? Big deal! I've seen that one lots of times in the cartoons and comics and stuff. It's an old joke. I thought the whole thing was boring. Did I miss something or what?"

LaShaun started to say that it wasn't the shoe that was important but what might have been *in* the shoe,

19

but he never said it because breakfast was interrupted by a loud crash and a loud "Damn!" Everyone turned and there was Fil, standing where he had dropped his breakfast all over the floor, now covered with broken china and slabs of sticky, syrupy pancakes. The whole room broke out in laughter as Fil bent over and started cleaning up the mess.

Without even wondering why he did it, LaShaun ran over, helped Fil pick up what was left of the plates and put the pieces on a tray. One of the kitchen staff brought a mop and bucket of warm water and cleaned up what was left on the floor. It was all over in just a minute or two but LaShaun noticed that Fil didn't go back for more pancakes and that he quietly left the Dining Hall looking embarrassed.

After breakfast, Worthy announced that two of the boys' cabins would team up with two of the girl's cabins and go for a short hike and tour of the campgrounds. The other two boys' cabins would play softball and the other two girls' cabins would play volleyball. After an hour or so the cabin groups would switch around. This way everybody would get a chance to meet each other.

The Elijah cabin was paired with the Judith cabin for the hike. Tracy, the girls cabin counselor, walked together with Fil out in front, but the boys and girls kept themselves as far from each other as possible.

They started the hike by walking past the Camp Office building where the director lived with his wife and then up the hill behind it. The ground was made up of a mixture of red dirt and white granite sand. Most of the area was covered with trees. Tracy said the scraggly ones with needles were scrub, or Digger Pine, the trees with regular leaves were live oak and the really tall trees with large, long pinecones were Sugar Pines.

At the top of the hill was a cross and a view down to the lake. To the east, they could see some of the granite mountains where the High Sierra rose up. Some of them still had snow on them from the previous winter.

On the way down, where there weren't trees there were thick, scratchy bushes called Manzanita. Fil told them not to eat the hard, round, green berries or they would get sick. Some of the bigger boys picked the berries and threw them at the back of the other kids' necks when Fil and Tracy weren't looking.

When they got to the lake there were willows growing along the shore. There were also lots of granite boulders. Some of them were quite large, like the one LaShaun had sat behind and cried when his father had left him at camp the day before.

Behind the boys' cabins was a large flat area with grass where there was a volleyball net, a basketball court, horseshoe pits, a softball field and a large tent with three ping-pong tables underneath. The equipment could be signed out from a small shed. Everywhere around the camp there were small clusters of log seats or picnic tables for the different cabin groups to use during their study and craft activities.

At the lake there was a gravelly beach with a cluster of ten or so brightly-colored two-person kayaks. Each kayak had two sets of paddles and two life jackets. There was a long rope held up by small white buoys that looped out into the water where it marked the area where swimming was allowed. In the middle of that area was a floating wooden platform the kids could swim to, lie in the sun or dive from.

There was also a large sign that said, "Water Safety Rules." Rule Number One: "God loves you!" Rule Number Two: "Swimming allowed only during designated times when lifeguard is on duty." Rule Number Three: "Kayaks may be checked out for use by those who have successfully completed the 'Kayaking and Water Safety class."

For non-swimmers there was a "Beginning Swim and Water Safety Class." Since LaShaun had never learned how to swim, his father had signed him up for the swimming class. The class was held for an hour every afternoon at the swimming pool behind the Dining Hall.

There were a few birds, too. Fil pointed out that the loud, squawking ones with the pointed tufts of feathers on their heads were Steller's Jays, "Or," he added, "you can just call them Blue Jays like most people do."

He also pointed out two Gray Squirrels up in a tree and some Chipmunks that liked to hang around the picnic tables closest to the Dining Hall and the Snack Shack down by the beach.

Fil said that sometimes, especially in the evening, there were deer and once, the year before, some of the kids had seen a bear walking through the girl's cabins during the night. Tracy interrupted to say they shouldn't worry about the bears. They should just follow the rule not to have any food in their cabin and, if they ever saw a bear, they should quietly turn and walk in the opposite direction and tell one of the camp staff.

LaShaun enjoyed the hike but after a while, he started to spend more of his time watching one of the girls, who seemed to be glancing at him every so often, too. He heard one of the other girls call her Marcy and, although she probably was not aware of it yet, she was becoming pretty . . . at least this is what LaShaun thought she was.

He began to daydream that they became friends before the week was over but, like getting dressed in front of everyone else, deep down he didn't really think this was going to happen either. At least not yet; not this summer.

After the hike was over all the kids had juice, fruit and cookies outside the Dining Hall.

When they were finished with the snacks, the Elijah boys played softball against the Moses boys and the Judith girls played volleyball against the Lydia cabin. Even though he was not as big as some of the other boys, LaShaun was good at softball. He played shortstop and actually threw out five boys at first base during the game.

Mo also turned out to be a good softball player. He hit one pitch all the way into the volleyball court for a home run. LaShaun figured it probably had something to do with his grandfather being a baseball coach. He secretly hoped the boys wouldn't have to play volleyball because he wasn't very good at it.

During the game, he heard some of the bigger boys on his team talking about what a loser Fil was.

"Why did we have to get stuck with such a jerk" was how one of them put it.

"He talks like a fool and he can't even carry his breakfast without dropping it on the floor."

"Yeah, and that story he told last night was dumb, too. I don't even know how he got to be a counselor at the camp. Don't they have to pass a test or something?"

LaShaun listened but didn't say anything even though he didn't agree with them. There was something about Fil that he liked. He felt as though Fil would listen and understand if he ever felt like talking to him about . . . well . . . about the things he might talk to him about if they ever talked.

The camp bell rang and the softball game just stopped where it was. After a bathroom break and a chance to wash their hands, it was time to have lunch in the Dining Hall.

Chapter Three
Quite a Story
Monday Afternoon

Some of LaShaun's shyness had worn off so he and Mo sat and ate with two of the smaller boys in their cabin—Phil, who played the piano and Colin, who had been to Europe and was sleeping on a lower bunk next to LaShaun. While they ate peanut butter and jelly or tuna sandwiches, LaShaun shared that he lived in a place called San Rafael and Phil shared that he and Glen lived in Sacramento and went to the same church. Three of the girls at camp also went to their church but when LaShaun asked, Phil said none of them was named Marcy.

The kids spent the hour after lunch on "electives," special activities they had signed up for in advance. There was a "Sports" elective where kids learned archery, horseshoes, ping-pong, rope climbing and

Frisbee golf. There was a "Camp Craft" elective with tent-building, cooking over a campfire, knife and axe skills, back-packing, and fishing. There was a "Creative Writing" class with a focus on short stories and poetry. There was a "Music" elective with a focus on composing and singing; and there was the "Beginner Swimming" elective LaShaun had joined.

LaShaun surprised himself by changing into his swimsuit in the cabin right out in the open and then headed for the pool. The electives were open to boys and girls and LaShaun was both happy and nervous when he saw that Marcy was in the pool waiting for the class to start.

During class, the teacher had all the kids get into the water. They played "Marco Polo" and put their heads under water. She then showed them how to float on their backs and had them choose partners to help each other practice. Most of the kids knew someone else in the class and partners were chosen so quickly LaShaun was left looking around without one. Marcy hadn't found a partner either, so when she saw LaShaun standing alone she waded over and asked if she could be his partner.

She said her name was Marcy and LaShaun pretended that he didn't know it already. He said his name was LaShaun and Marcy said she already knew his name from when Fil had thanked him for helping clean up the mess in the Dining Hall that morning.

Each of them helped hold the other up as they practiced floating on their backs. Marcy floated easily but LaShaun's feet kept sinking until the teacher came over and told him to stretch his arms out farther above his head. LaShaun was convinced this would make his head sink but he tried it and found he could float almost as well as Marcy.

He had been very hesitant to touch Marcy on her back as she lay in the water until she said, "What are you doing, LaShaun? Keep me up!" He noticed Marcy didn't hesitate to touch him and her hands felt like the touch of angels on his back. The thought crossed his mind that even if he had been in the creative writing class, he wouldn't have known how to describe the feeling with words.

When the electives were over everyone had free time for an hour and half. Some kids checked out basketballs and ping pong paddles. Others had signed up for the kayak safety training class. Others swam and played in the lake or in the pool. LaShaun went down to the lake and waded in the cold water, wondering if he would be able to swim out to the diving platform before he went home on Saturday morning. He wondered if he and Marcy would swim out to it together.

When the camp bell rang, everyone went back to his or her cabin to change and have afternoon group time. Fil told his boys they had five minutes to find a rock and come back to tell a story about it. The story was to be at least one minute long but not longer than three. As usual, the bigger boys all looked at each other and groaned. LaShaun thought it sounded like it might be fun so he was the first one out of the cabin and the first one back. The rock he found was a small, smooth one about the size of a thimble. It was bluish-black in color with small veins of reddish-orange running through it.

When it came time to tell their stories Fil began by reading Jesus' parable of the lost coin from Luke 15.

After reading it, Fil said, "Imagine if the coin had been a rock instead of a coin. For Jesus, a rock would have been an easy thing to use in telling a story about God or about the kingdom of Heaven. Let's see what stories your rocks have to tell."

He asked Marty, one of the bigger boys, to start first. Marty held up a crumbly, non-descript chunk of granite that looked as though it had been the first rock he had seen lying on the ground.

"This is my rock," he said. "It used to be a baseball but then a wizard turned it into a fairy princess who married a frog who kissed her and turned her into this rock. She used to wear a golden crown but when she turned into a rock it fell off."

The other big boys laughed and one of them shouted out, "Good story, Marty!" and "You should turn it into a book!"

Marty's story had taken less than thirty seconds but Fil didn't seem to notice.

Instead, he said, "Good job, Marty. I especially liked the part about the crown. That was very creative."

He paused for a moment before saying, "Okay, who wants to go next."

LaShaun was having trouble thinking up a story for his rock.

When no one else raised their hand Fil said, "How about you, LaShaun, tell us your story."

LaShaun started to say he didn't have one. But when he opened his mouth, a story started to come out if it instead.

"Once there was a boy . . . about our age . . . who lived with his parents on a small farm high on a mountain and deep in a forest. He didn't have any brothers or sisters and didn't have any friends to play with after school because he lived so far away from everyone else.

"After he finished his homework and chores each day, he would walk to the nearby places that were special to him. There was a fallen tree near the creek where he could sit in the warm sun and listen to the sound of the rushing water. There was a meadow where he could try and catch the butterflies and bees that landed on the beautiful wildflowers. There was a spot a little way up the mountain where he could dangle his legs over the edge and imagine he could see places like Japan or Egypt or Jerusalem shimmering in the haze along the distant horizon.

"But his favorite place of all was an old oak tree on the edge of the clearing behind the barn. It wasn't a thin, pukey oak tree like the ones around here, but a big one like you might find in a place like Mirkwood or Sherwood Forest."

LaShaun noticed that some of the bigger boys were yawning or pretending to yawn. Others were rolling their eyes, but he also noticed that several of the smaller boys were nodding their heads as if they knew something about what he was talking about.

"The tree had a small, secret hole in it where an owl might have lived. But there wasn't an owl in it. Instead it was the place where the boy hid his treasures. His most precious treasure was a small rock that looked exactly like this one."

He held up his rock again so everyone could see it.

"When the boy held it in his hand and rubbed it between his finger and thumb the rock would get

31

warm and begin to glow. He had learned that if he made a wish when the stone was glowing the brightest, his wish would sometimes be granted . . . but not always.

"Once he wished he could fly. He had hoped he would sprout wings but no wings sprouted. Instead, he took a deep breath, and when he began to let out a disappointed sigh, he found himself rising off the ground until he was higher than the barn and then higher than all but the highest trees. He could make himself move forward or turn one way or the other simply by thinking it to himself."

LaShaun paused again, and noticed the older boys weren't acting like they were bored any more. They were all looking at him and listening like the younger ones.

"One day," LaShaun continued, "the boy's father became very sick. He was so sick his mother took him to the hospital in the big city. The boy stayed with his aunt and uncle who lived just off the highway about halfway to the hospital. The boy took the rock with him and rubbed it and rubbed it until the skin on his finger and thumb began to get red and raw. Over and over again he wished for his father to get well and to come home, but two days later the phone rang. It was his mother and she told him his father had died.

"The boy cried and, when he had finished crying, he went outside. He took the rock out of his pocket and threw it as hard and as far away as he could. He then went back inside, sat down and put his head on his aunt's lap. His mother came back the next day. They got their things from the farm and moved in with the aunt and uncle. He never saw the farm again.

"Years later, when he was a man, his mother died. When he was cleaning out her home, he found an old pair of jeans rolled up inside one of the cardboard boxes in the attic. They looked about the size of jeans a twelve-year old boy might wear. As he was rolling them up to put them back in the box, he felt a hard lump somewhere inside the jeans. Inside one of the pockets, he found the rock he thought he had thrown away so many years before. This is, "LaShaun said as he held up the rock for a third time, "not just *like* that rock . . ." He paused for a moment and then with some emotion, said, "This *is* that rock."

LaShaun's eyes closed and his arms dropped limp to his sides. A few seconds later, his eyes opened again. To Fil and to the other boys, LaShaun looked as though he had suddenly awakened from a trance and maybe they were right to think it; for LaShaun felt as though he had just lived through a dream that had spoken itself through his mouth without him having very much to do with any of it.

33

No one said a word so he stuck the rock in his pocket, walked back to the group, sat down on the ground and waited for the next boy to come up and tell a story. But no one did. And Fil didn't ask anyone to come up.

Instead, Fil said, "Uh . . . that was quite a story you just told us, LaShaun. It might be the best story I have ever heard anyone tell up here at camp."

Fil swallowed hard as though his mouth had become dry.

"I'm sure the rest of you also have some good stories to tell about your rocks but maybe we can . . . uh . . . maybe we might just wait to . . . you know . . . wait to hear them later, okay?"

A couple of the boys managed to say, "Sure, Fil. That's all right with us."

One or two of the boys might have been disappointed that they weren't able to tell their story but the rest, whether they would admit it out loud or not, were glad they didn't have to tell one, especially after hearing LaShaun's. It had been too good.

"Free time," Fil announced, "until the dinner bell rings."

Everyone wandered away except for LaShaun.

Fil walked over to him, sat down and asked, "That was some story you just told us. Can you tell me . . . uh

. . . no . . . I mean . . . are you able to tell me where that story came from and what it was all about?"

LaShaun listened to the question and wondered if he knew the answer.

After thinking about it for a while he said, "I don't know where it came from. I never heard it before . . . and . . . ," he stopped to choose his words carefully, "I don't think I made it up, either. It just sort of showed up on its own."

Fil nodded silently as if he knew exactly what LaShaun was talking about.

"Yes, but do you know if it meant anything? . . . I mean . . . did it mean anything to you?"

LaShaun sat quietly for a long time trying to decide whether to say what he was thinking or not. After thinking about it he decided to only share one part of it.

"I think," he said, "it had something to do with prayer . . . I think."

Fil guessed there was more to LaShaun's story than that but he could tell LaShaun was being honest when he said it had something to do with prayer.

"Like I said just before you told your story, Jesus used to tell stories too. I think your story was one Jesus could have told. I think maybe your story was a sort of parable about prayer."

LaShaun nodded his head and, still thinking about what had just happened, turned and walked back to the cabin where he tried to write down everything he could remember about his story in his bedtime journal. He hadn't even come close to finishing when the dinner bell rang.

Chapter Four
A Story Without Words
Monday Evening

LaShaun hurried over to the bathroom, washed his hands and almost ran to catch up with the others who were already standing in line to pick up their dinner from the kitchen staff.

After getting his food, he sat down with Mo, Colin and Phil but nobody said much to him while they ate. The other boys talked about how fun their electives were and what they did during their afternoon recreation time. LaShaun started to say something about his swimming class but thinking about the swimming class made him think of Marcy and thinking about Marcy made him think that maybe he wouldn't say anything at all. So, he just listened to the other boys and ate his spaghetti, garlic toast and salad, keeping his mouth full so he wouldn't blurt out something he would be embarrassed about.

At the evening campfire circle, Tracy gave a short devotion about the time Jesus told his disciples to cast their nets over on the other side of their boat.

"Sometimes," she said, "when we try to do the same thing over and over again the same way without any success, we should try to do it a different way and 'cast our nets' in a different direction.

"Some people who are looking for God try to find God in nature, in science, in philosophy, in famous people, in doing good things for other people, in protecting the environment and in lots of different religions.

"People," she said, "will try to find God everywhere and anywhere except in Jesus. Why they do this, I don't understand.

"When I finally did get around to looking for God in Jesus, I found what I was looking for. It was just like Jesus said, 'He who has seen me has seen the Father. For I and the Father are one.'

"So," she said at the end, "if you are looking for God and not finding him maybe you need to start throwing your net over on the other side of the boat. On the Jesus side of the boat."

When Tracy was finished Worthy stood up with her guitar and led everyone in singing some praise and worship songs. This time, there were two other counselors who played their guitars along with her. LaShaun enjoyed all of it but when Tracy was giving her devotion, he kept wondering if, when the disciples pulled in their nets with all the fish in them, there was a shoe in there somewhere.

One of the other counselors gave a closing prayer and everyone slowly walked back to their cabins.

After they were back at the cabin, but before they had changed and gotten ready for bed, Fil took all the boys to a place where there was no sign of the electric lights that went on each evening at sunset all around the camp. He had the boys turn off their flashlights and lie flat on their backs looking straight up at the nighttime sky. The sky was filled with stars that most of them had never seen before because they lived in places where there were so many lights that the stars weren't bright enough to compete with them.

As they lay there, Fil said, from memory, the opening words of Psalm 19:

The heavens declare the glory of God;
    the skies proclaim the work of his hands.
Day after day, they pour forth speech;
    night after night they reveal knowledge.

They have no speech, they use no words;
    no sound is heard from them.
Yet their voice goes out into all the earth,
    their words to the ends of the world.

After a little while, Fil spoke again. "We've all . . . uh . . . heard some stories from each other since we got here yesterday. We've heard some stories from the Bible, especially some from Jesus. I told you last night . . . I mean a story . . . I mean I told you a story last night and . . . uh . . . we all heard LaShaun tell his story this afternoon. Right now, before we go to bed, I want you to listen to the story that the stars are telling you. The Bible says they are telling us something about God. Listen carefully, because whatever you hear is what I want you to write down in your bed-time journal tonight."

Later, after everyone was in bed, LaShaun tried to write down the rest of his story and never got around to writing down what the stars had told him.

After Fil said "Good night" and flipped off the lights, someone said, "Hey Fil, tell us another story!"

The voice of one of the bigger boys said, in what sounded like a mocking tone of voice, "No! We want LaShaun to tell us a story."

"Yeah," said another voice, "tell us a story, LaShaun. I bet you can't tell one as good as the one you told this afternoon!"

LaShaun didn't know what to say or what to do so he was glad when Fil interrupted and said, "No. I think LaShaun already told us a good story today. If you want, I'll tell you one."

The smaller kids all said, "Yes, please. Tell us a story."

Even one of the bigger boys said, "Go on, Fil. Tell us a story if you feel you have to."

So, Fil told a story.

"Just down the freeway from here is a town called Auburn. Auburn grew from nothing into a small city during the California gold rush beginning in 1849. Among the many men trying to make their fortunes from mining and panning gold were two friends that people called 'Bent-Pan Billy' and 'Lucky Lars.' Billy's name was sort of self-explanatory but it's hard to figure out how Lars got his.

"I mean Lars had never really been lucky at much of anything. Back home in Indiana he had tried his hand at farming but, just before harvest, his crops caught fire and burned up. Then, after he moved to Missouri, he tried raising cattle but his first, small herd was stolen by two cattle rustlers. The men were later caught and hung but not until they had slaughtered the herd and sold off the meat. Lars was completely broke when he heard that gold had been discovered in California.

"When he got to Auburn, he met a man named Billy. Now Billy was just the opposite of Lars. Everything that he had ever done had turned out well. But after his wife died of Scarlet Fever he had just

41

given up and quit doing much of anything. The news of the gold rush offered him a reason to keep on living so, like Lars, he found himself in Auburn.

"The things they needed to help them find gold were so expensive that neither Lars nor Billy could afford to buy everything they needed. So, they got together and decided if they put their money together, they could afford to buy it all. So, they bought some shovels, a pick axe, some gold pans, a sluice box, some buckets and two small kegs of dynamite in case they needed to blast through some rock. They already had a canvas tent, some blankets for sleeping and some pots and pans for cooking their food."

Phil interrupted the story by asking, "What about food? Didn't they need food?"

"Shut up," someone said. "Just let him tell the story."

Fil let the awkward moment pass before he continued with the story.

"For a long time, they couldn't find a place to dig for gold because other miners had already staked claims everywhere they went. Finally, when they were just about ready to give up and quit, they found an unclaimed section along Gold Creek, just up the hill above what's now the Bible Camp.

"They dug down in the rocky ground and, at first, sifted water through the dirt and gravel in their pans.

They found some gold dust and a few small nuggets but not enough to make a living. So, they set up their sluice box and started digging deeper into the ground.

"Billy did most of the digging and Lars ran the sluice box, making sure that there was enough water running through it to separate out any gold or gold ore from the rest of the dirt and gravel. Soon the creek was surrounded by large piles of all the dirt and gravel that had been sifted out.

The story was interrupted a second time when someone yelled, "Stop kicking me, you big jerk," and, "Keep your feet to yourself."

The room became filled with the voices of boys yelling, "Quiet!" "Shhh," "Knock it off," and "Cut it out."

As before, Fil waited until the room was quiet before picking up where he had left off.

"After several weeks they temporarily closed up camp and went down to Grass Valley to sell their gold and buy some more food. Before they left, Lars took the two kegs of dynamite, wrapped them in a waterproof oilskin cloth and buried them next to a granite boulder.

"Although Lars later denied it, some folks said the two of them brought a small fortune in gold back to Grass Valley that day.

"The way Lars told it, after three days in Grass Valley Billy left town and headed back to camp by himself. When Lars got there two days later, he couldn't find Billy anywhere. When he went to dig up the dynamite, he found nothing there except for a large hole the ground. After looking around he found Billy's pick axe stuck half-way up the trunk of a nearby Sugar Pine. Billy's gold pan was lying behind the boulder, all bent-up just like his name, and part-way down the hill he found what looked like a piece of the fancy belt buckle Billy was wearing the day he left Grass Valley to go back to the camp.

"Lars began telling the other miners that Billy must have started digging a new hole with his pick axe and accidently stuck it into one of the kegs of dynamite and that must have been the end of Billy. But other people said they hadn't heard the dynamite explode until after Lars had come back to the camp and still other people wondered if maybe they had found so much gold Lars figured this was his chance to be really lucky for once and had blown up Billy so he could keep it all for himself.

The room was now completely silent as the boys waited to hear what happened next.

"One night a group of vigilantes came into the camp, grabbed Lars and took him down to Auburn to be put on trial for murder. Lars, of course, denied all

44

of it and said they hadn't really found very much gold at all.

"As one of the witnesses put it in Lars' defense, 'There ain't been any of Billy's body parts found anywhere so who's sayin' that he's really dead for sure or not?'

"The jury, which was made up mostly of other miners, had seen too much of arguing and feuding between partners before and they knew that, in a moment of drunken confusion, it was all too easy for one man to strike down and kill a man who had, until that very moment, been his best friend.

"When the verdict came in it was unanimous: 'Guilty as charged.' The next day Lars was strung up on the well-used tree in the town square and hung by the neck until dead, just like the men who had stolen Billy's cattle back in Missouri.

"That would be the end of the story except for a couple of things. The first thing is that with both mining partners dead their claim was free to be picked up by someone else. It was, in fact, picked up by the man who had been the foreman of the jury that had convicted Lars.

The man found a lot of gold on the claim. He eventually became very wealthy and built a small mansion in San Francisco, on California Street just down from the top of Nob Hill.

"The second thing was a rumor; a rumor that was confirmed by a number of men who claimed to have been in the Red Eye Saloon in Grass Valley several days after Lars had been hung and buried in Auburn. According to these men someone who looked exactly like Bent-Pan Billy walked into the saloon and ordered a shot of whiskey. After downing the whiskey, he reached into his pocket, pulled out a nugget of gold the size of a ping pong ball and set it down on the bar.

"'That oughta be more than enough to pay for the whiskey,' he said. 'And,' he added, 'you can keep the change.'

"He then walked out of the bar and the men rushed out to see where he was going but when they stepped outside, he was nowhere to be seen. Another miner, who had been sitting outside the saloon door keeping an eye on his mule, swore no one had gone into the bar or come out of it the whole time he had been sitting there. But the gold nugget was real and worth a small fortune.

"Some folks told how the man who jumped the claim had trouble with things mysteriously disappearing from the site and his equipment kept breaking down at the worst possible times. Other folks wondered if maybe Billy and Lars, alive or dead, were in some way responsible for the fire that later destroyed that small mansion in San Francisco . . . a fire that also took the life of the greedy jury foreman.

"Oh . . . and one more thing . . . Several times since I've been up here at the camp, late at night, I have heard what sounded like a small bomb going off somewhere up the hill where the creek comes down towards the lake. Other camp staff who heard the same noise said it was just the sound of thunder. But I remember seeing the sky full of stars each time and have never been convinced it was thunder that I heard."

There was a short pause. "Well, boys . . . that was a long story and more than enough talking for tonight. Now go to sleep."

And that was that.

Chapter Five

Juggling

Tuesday Morning

Tuesday morning began with the Day-Start Devotions. Phil was given the Bible verse to read and everyone was asked to think of some place they had been or seen in a picture, some place that the verse reminded them of. The verse was about Jesus feeding the crowd of five thousand people so most of the boys thought of places out in the country or where they had been on picnics. LaShaun remembered the bare hillsides on the ocean end of Muir Woods, just south of where he lived. The hillsides were covered with bright orange California Golden Poppies with views across the vast, blue Pacific Ocean far down below.

Before someone read the closing prayer, Fil said, "Wherever you are, Jesus will be there, too. All you have to do is remember to look for him."

After that they all got dressed and left to get breakfast.

At the Dining Hall Fil asked LaShaun if they could eat breakfast together and, of course, LaShaun said yes.

As they were eating their scrambled eggs and sausage, LaShaun asked Fil why he had left the Dining Hall after dropping his breakfast all over the floor the day before.

"You are always saying or doing things wrong but that was the first time you looked embarrassed about anything."

Fil considered how to answer the question but, in the end, he decided to be honest about it.

"I wasn't embarrassed about dropping the food on the floor. I do stuff like that all the time. I don't want to do it but it just seems to happen to me. I was embarrassed because . . . well . . . I was embarrassed because I said the word, 'Damn' out loud for everyone in the room to hear. This is supposed to be a Bible Camp and because I am a counselor, I am supposed to be an example to everyone . . . you know . . . like what a follower of Jesus is supposed to be like. It just didn't seem right for me to be saying . . . you know . . . that word in front of everybody."

LaShaun nodded his head and said, "That's okay. I'm supposed to be a Christian and sometimes I say that word, too. I don't want to say it but it just comes out. Once I even heard our pastor say some bad words next to the office copier when he didn't think anyone could hear him. I figured he was just having a bad day and it didn't seem as though it had much to do with Jesus at all."

This time it was Fil's turn to nod his head.

He said, "I hope everyone else feels the same way about it that you do. But I doubt it."

Then he added, "Hey, I almost forgot the reason I wanted to eat breakfast with you. It's about the story you told yesterday. You said you thought it was about prayer but you also . . . uh . . . looked as though there was more to it than that. You looked as though you wanted to tell me more. Is that right? There is . . . no, I mean . . . *is* there something else you want to talk about?"

LaShaun quietly nodded his head again and said in a very quiet whisper, "Yes, but I don't want to talk about it here with everybody listening."

So, Fil suggested that maybe they could talk during the afternoon free time and LaShaun said that would be good.

After breakfast, Worthy paired up each boy's cabin group with a girl's cabin like she had done the day before. This time the Elijah cabin was matched with the Sarah cabin and they had to play volleyball against each other. Two other groups played softball and the other four groups went off to do something else.

With eight boys or girls on a team it was hard to hit the ball over the net without hitting someone on the head. But both teams kept missing the ball most of the time. LaShaun only hit the ball back over the net once the whole time. He decided he now hated volleyball even more than he had before, especially after Sarah beat Elijah three times in a row.

After the volleyball and softball games were finished the four cabin groups headed down to the Dining Hall where they found the usual snacks waiting for them. On the way, they passed the other four groups who were on their way to play softball and volleyball against each other.

One of the groups was the Judith cabin. LaShaun knew this because he saw Marcy. Marcy saw him, too, and gave him a big smile and a little wave as they went off in opposite directions. LaShaun smiled back at her but was too embarrassed to wave.

After standing around and eating cookies for a few minutes Fil stood up and said, "Time to go, Elijah guys. Follow me down the Yellow Brick Road to the wonderful city of Oz!"

Most of the boys had no idea what he was talking about and some of them figured it was just one more example of how much of an idiot he was. LaShaun, however, not only knew about the movie but thought he knew what Fil meant by what he said about the Yellow Brick Road and Oz. Oz, he figured, was where Fil was going to take them and the Yellow Brick Road was the way they were going to get there.

As they followed Fil down towards the lake, they were joined by the three other cabin groups they had been with all morning.

When they came to the large campfire circle LaShaun half-expected to find a "wonderful wizard" standing nearby. There wasn't a wizard but there was a man standing in the middle of the circle juggling three rocks the size of golf balls. LaShaun imagined the man really was a wizard and that he was going to turn each of the rocks into a princess like in the story Marty had told the day before.

The counselors told everyone to sit and the man started to talk while he juggled.

"Sometimes," he said, "there are a lot of things going on in our lives. And sometimes we do not feel as though we can handle them all. For me, juggling three rocks is easy."

He did a few trick moves like flinging one of the rocks up from behind his back and another one from between his legs.

"But there are times when life becomes even harder for us."

And here he nodded at Fil who picked up another rock and tossed it in the air towards the man. The man caught the rock without missing a beat and continued to juggle all four rocks in a new pattern that seemed very complicated to LaShaun.

As he watched, LaShaun started thinking about his life back home. He had to admit there were a lot of things he had been juggling, too. Sometimes it was easy, just like the man said, and sometimes it was hard. He could think of a lot of times when he had "dropped the ball" just like the man had just done with one of the rocks.

"Sometimes we simply can't keep the juggling act going and we mess it up," the man said as he picked the rock back up and started juggling again. "This can make us feel like we have failed to get everything right the way we want it to be."

Here he nodded to Fil who tossed a fifth rock into the air. The man caught it and for a few moments managed to keep all five up in the air at the same time. But then one dropped to the ground and then another and then he had to duck as a third rock narrowly missed hitting him in the head.

"I am a good juggler and I can keep four things up in the air at the same time . . . most of the time. But I am not good enough to keep five things up in the air for very long."

"What do you think? Does this make me a bad juggler?"

The boys all yelled back, "No!"

"Does it make me a failure?"

Once again, the boys shouted, "No!"

"Of course, it doesn't make me a failure because I have practiced and practiced to do the best juggling I can do. And life is like that. Sometimes our lives become so difficult we want to give up . . . because we can't keep it all going at the same time anymore."

LaShaun listened very carefully, because he was convinced he was a failure, too; just like his father and just like his mother.

He had heard his father recently say, "LaShaun, I don't think I can take this for much longer. Something is going to have to give or else I am going to give up."

For LaShaun this had been a hard thing for him to hear. He knew his father had been working two jobs to pay the bills and that he was trying to spend all his free time with LaShaun so he could take him places and help him with his homework. But there was shopping and housecleaning and going to church and bills to pay and LaShaun had begun to think that maybe he was like the fifth rock his father could no longer keep up in the air. Maybe it was because of him that everything was about to come crashing to the ground.

LaShaun felt like he had been juggling too many things in his own life, too, and he wasn't sure he could keep it up much longer. He had convinced himself he had to keep doing everything perfectly for the sake of his father. He felt that if he couldn't get good grades and do all his chores and be patient when his father wasn't being patient he would have failed. The thought of this had been haunting him for a long time. He even had nightmares about things like jumping off of a high diving board and missing the water or sitting down at a piano in front of hundreds of people and then forgetting the music he was supposed to play.

But this man—this juggler—had said that just because a person can't do everything, that doesn't make them a failure. LaShaun wondered if this could be true?

"You see," the man said, "we all have Sin in our bodies. By Sin I don't mean the bad things we do or the mistakes we make. These are things that the Bible calls 'sins.' Sin, however, isn't the bad things we do, it is the weak part in us that makes it impossible for us to do the right thing every time, all the time. Sin puts a limit on how good we can be. It is, sadly, the way we are and we can't get rid of it. Sometimes Sin makes us feel like failures, too. But God says 'No' to Sin and 'Yes' to you and to me.

"The Bible says 'God so loved the world that he gave his only Son; that whoever believes in him should not perish but have everlasting life.'

"I bet most of you know that verse and some of you have probably memorized it." LaShaun nodded his head because he had memorized the verse in Sunday school.

"But," the man continued, "I doubt that any of you have memorized the verse that comes right after it: John 3:17.

"The verse goes like this: 'For God did not send his Son into the world to condemn the world but that the world, through him, might be saved.'

"Jesus came to die for both our sins and for our Sin. Because of Jesus, God can forgive us for all of it. It's as if God is saying, 'The reason I don't condemn you is because I love you so much.' God asks us to do our very best and then promises to help us with the things that are too hard for us to handle by ourselves. Sometimes God does this by sending his Holy Spirit to make things work out. Other times God helps us by sending a friend to help us . . . or a doctor . . . or a counselor.

"The Bible says that 'God is *for* us,' not against us. God loves you just the way you are. And God looks forward to what you will become when you grow up; when he will see you doing everything you can to be the best follower of Jesus you can possibly be.

The man picked up four rocks and started juggling them again. "God doesn't think of you as being a failure. So, don't ever think of yourself as being one.

"Juggling is not always easy and life is not always easy, either. But with God's help we will be able to get through even the worse times in our lives."

And then, one by one, he tossed the rocks onto the ground in the middle of the circle.

Fil said, "Let's give Mr. Lee a big hand. Isn't he amazing?"

And of course, all the boys and girls clapped and cheered for Mr. Lee. Some of it was because of what he had said. But most of the applause was simply because everyone likes to see a juggler!

When everyone stopped clapping the counselors opened up a large container filled with hacky-sacks and had each boy or girl in their group come up and take three of them. After everyone had their hacky-sacks they were told to try juggling them like Mr. Lee. Only a few boys were able to do it for even a few times. The rest were throwing the sacks all over the place and trying to catch them before they hit the ground. Everyone was laughing because it was so funny.

Mr. Lee interrupted the juggling to add one more thought.

"You see how much fun you are having trying to juggle those hacky-sacks? I bet that not one of you feels like a failure because you can't do it. This is how it should be with you at church. No one is perfect there, either. But everyone is trying to do their best for Jesus. In church, you should be laughing all the time both for the things you do right and for the things that don't turn out so well. And the reason you should laugh is because God is so happy for you that he is laughing too! And don't forget . . . if you keep practicing, with God's help you become real juggler like me!"

The boys all clapped again. The cabin counselors had everyone put the hacky-sacks back in the container and then Mr. Lee picked it up and left.

Fil handed out paper and pencils to all of the Elijah boys and asked each of them to draw a picture of a time when they had felt bad because they had messed up.

After a few minutes he said, "Now write these words somewhere on the paper: 'God forgives me and that makes me feel very happy!' And," he added, "don't forget to put an exclamation mark at the end of that!"

LaShaun drew a picture of himself trying to juggle a zillion rocks all at the same time. The picture showed them falling like hailstones all around him with one bouncing off of his head. He wrote the word "Ouch" over his head and drew a little arrow from the word to his mouth. He looked at it for a moment and realized he had gotten it mixed up. The word wasn't supposed to be going *into* his mouth, it was supposed to be coming *out* of it! So, he erased the arrow and drew another one that went from his mouth to the word.

LaShaun did not draw very well but he liked this particular drawing. He liked it so much that after he had written the words about God forgiving him, he drew a big smile on his face. Fil said they could keep the picture but he wanted them to give the pencils back.

Then everyone rushed off to get ready for lunch except for LaShaun who walked over to Fil and said, "Now I think I know why you don't get all upset when you mess things up."

He paused for a moment and then gave his answer: "Because you know God forgives you, right?"

Fil just smiled and said, "You got it pal! Are we still on to meet during free time?"

LaShaun nodded and broke into a big smile, just like the one he had drawn on his picture. Then, without saying a word, he ran straight to the Dining Hall to eat lunch.

Chapter Six
Maybe It Was a Gift
Tuesday Afternoon

LaShaun thought it was wrong to have his swimming lesson so soon after he had eaten lunch. His father said this can give you cramps and then you might drown.

So, after lunch, LaShaun asked his swimming teacher about it and she said, "Swimming right after you have eaten does not give you cramps. But your father is right about one thing, if you eat too much you could cough some of it up and choke on it. That wouldn't be a good thing if you were swimming! But don't worry about it here," she said. "We are just practicing and learning how to swim. And I'm here to help you if you run into any trouble."

After this, LaShaun felt a little better about going into the pool right after lunch. But, to be on the safe side, he tried to eat as little lunch as possible for the rest of the week.

Today the class learned how to float on their stomachs. This was harder than floating on their backs because their faces were in the water most of the time. Both LaShaun and Marcy were able to float right away but LaShaun noticed that every time he tried to lift his head out of the water his legs began to sink. The teacher said that if he wanted to breathe, he should just turn his head to the side.

After everyone had practiced floating on their stomachs the teacher said, "Now you are almost ready to start swimming. Swimming, you see, is just floating on your stomach and paddling with your arms. So, we're half-way there!"

She then had the kids practice floating at the deep end of the pool, close to the edge where they could hold on if they needed to. Everyone in the class did this very well.

The next thing they had to do was jump into the deep water from the side of the pool, float on their backs, turn over onto their stomachs and then find some way to paddle their way over to the edge of the pool.

Some of the kids were afraid to jump into the water so the teacher said it was okay for them to just slip into the water while holding onto the edge. They did this one at a time and LaShaun tried hard not to laugh as he watched the kids flailing around and splashing the water as they tried to swim.

When it was his turn Marcy told him to "just do it and pretend I'm there to hold you up."

LaShaun jumped into the water. He forgot to float on his back and went straight to floating on his stomach. He reached one hand out to grab the edge of the pool but it was too far away, so he pulled that hand back and reached out with his other hand. He had to pull that one back, too. But when he reached the other hand out again, he found he had actually moved forward to where he could reach the edge of the pool easily.

He heard the teacher applaud and say, "LaShaun, that was wonderful. You actually swam to the edge of the pool! Well done!"

After class, when they were getting out of the pool, Marcy asked LaShaun if he would like to do something together with her during their free time. He started to say, "Yes," but he remembered he was supposed to meet with Fil.

"I can't today," he said, "but maybe we can do it tomorrow . . . if that's alright with you . . ."

Marcy said, "Okay," and LaShaun walked back to the cabin to change into his shorts and t-shirt.

Fil was waiting for him at the cabin. They walked down to the campfire circle where they had watched the juggler earlier in the day. LaShaun thought he would be nervous but was surprised to discover he was actually excited about the chance to talk to Fil about . . . well . . . about his family and the things that were worrying hm.

Fil started off by saying a short prayer asking God to bless their time together.

He then looked at LaShaun and said, "Go ahead, tell me what's on your mind. And don't worry, I won't say anything about it to anyone. This is all just between you and me . . . and God."

So LaShaun started talking and he didn't stop for nearly an hour. He talked about how his earliest memories were of his mother yelling at him and spanking him for being so "stupid." He noticed she only did this when his father was at work. He then told Fil that when he was nine years old the police came to his house, arrested his mother and took her away. LaShaun said he still wasn't sure why she had been arrested. He knew it had something to do with drugs, or maybe it was something else. As far as he was concerned it didn't really matter one way or the other. What mattered is that she wasn't at home anymore.

Every so often, his father took him to see her in the state prison. Sometimes she looked happy to see him. But other times she didn't seem to care whether he was there or not. When Fil asked LaShaun how this made him feel he said it made him feel angry. He was angry at the police for taking her away. He was angry at his father for the times he had yelled at his mother. Most of all, he was angry at his mother for the way she had gone about ruining her life along with everyone else's.

The one thing that kept him going was his father saying Bible things like, "With God, nothing will be impossible" and "I can do all things through him who gives me strength."

Talking about this reminded LaShaun what the juggling-man had said about God helping us when we cannot do everything by ourselves. He pulled the drawing he had made out of his pocket and began to explain it all to Fil. When he was done talking about that he talked about how his father was so stressed and worn out that he wanted to quit. Then, of course, he talked about how bad he felt about himself.

Fil sat there for a long time, just looking at the ground and thinking about what LaShaun had just said.

The silence made LaShaun feel uncomfortable so he said, "Fil? What do you think?"

Fil looked up and answered with a question of his own

"LaShaun, what do you think God thinks about all of this?"

LaShaun thought about this for a while.

When he was ready, he said, "I'm not sure. I think that maybe because he loves me that maybe God isn't happy when things aren't going the way they should. I guess God feels sad the way I do. And maybe God is angry about all of this like I am.

Fil?" he asked. "Do you think God gets angry about things like this?"

"Yes, I think he does," Fil said. "Otherwise God wouldn't step in to help us get through times like that. There is a verse in the Bible that says something like this: 'God works for the good in all things, for those who love him and are called according to his purpose.' What that tells me is that God is more powerful than the bad thing and can help us to make something good come out of it."

LaShaun said, "I think I get it. It's sort of like taking a lemon and making lemonade, right?"

"Yes, I think that is exactly what it means. So then, what good things can you think of that can come out your situation?"

"I don't know," LaShaun said. "That's a hard one. Maybe one good thing is that I'm really close to my

Dad. I mean he really cares for me and would do anything for me. That's a good thing. And now that I know how hard it is then maybe I can help out some other kids who are having a hard time. That would be a good thing, too, wouldn't it?"

Fil looked as though what LaShaun said had caught him by surprise. Then he looked as though he wasn't there at all, even though his body hadn't moved.

"Fil?" LaShaun asked. "Are you all right?"

"What did you say?" Fil asked. "Oh . . . right . . . uh . . . yes, I'm all right.

"I was just thinking . . . I think you're right about being able to help other people who are hurting like you have been hurting. I think you'd be able to tell them that you got through it and if you could do it then they could too. Maybe you could do this is by telling stories. God has given you a real gift. I think God could use that gift to do a lot of good for . . . you know . . . for people."

LaShaun thought about it. He didn't have a brother or a sister and he had never had anyone to tell stories to until this week at camp. He really liked the way Fil told stories and he still couldn't understand how he was able to tell such a good one yesterday. Maybe it was God who told the story. Maybe it *was* sort of a gift . . .

Fil stood up and so did LaShaun.

"It's getting late and I have to get back for our afternoon group time. Thanks for being so honest with me, LaShaun. It makes me feel special to think that you'd trust me enough to tell me . . . what you just told me. Before we go, I'd like to say a prayer."

He put his hand on LaShaun's shoulder and said, "Lord, thank you for helping LaShaun get through this hard time. Maybe he wouldn't have gotten this far if you hadn't been loving him and helping him even when he didn't know it. Now help him to find the good things you have for him and . . . and . . . bless his father and mother during the hard times they are going through, too. Amen."

As they walked back to the cabin the camp bell rang. LaShaun felt good about his talk with Fil. If it was possible, the smile on his face was even bigger than before. He was really glad his father had signed him up for church camp! Back at the cabin, some of the boys had to change so LaShaun and the others ran over to the basketball court and shot baskets with some of the small pinecones that were lying all over the camp. It wasn't long before they heard Fil's voice call out, "C'mon you guys, it's time for Elijah to roll!" As they ran back to the cabin to join the rest of the group, they threw their pinecones at the trees, scoring points when they hit.

Fil walked with them up Gold Creek and around a bunch of Manzanita bushes. There were two old, weather-beaten picnic tables hidden behind the bushes in a place none of the boys had ever seen before.

"It's a secret spot only a few of the other counselor's know about. So," he said, "since it's a secret, let's all keep it a secret!"

He had them all "cross my heart and hope to die" before he would let them sit.

Then Fil said, "What I just had you say and do is sort of superstitious but it also has something to do with being a follower of Jesus. Can you guess why?"

Phil raised his hand and said, "Because we said, 'hope to die?' Isn't that like Jesus? We want to die like Jesus?"

"Well," Fil said slowly. "That isn't really what I had in mind. What I was thinking about was the 'cross my heart' part. I read there was a time that, when Christians made a promise to somebody, they would make the sign of the cross over their heart and then say they would rather die than break the promise. That's what it means to say, 'Cross my heart and hope to die.'

"But Jesus didn't teach his disciples to do things like that. What Jesus taught them was this . . ." And here he pulled out his pocket Bible, turned to Matthew 5:33-37 and read,

And Jesus said,

"You have heard that it was said to the people long ago, 'Do not break your oath, but fulfill to the Lord the vows you have made.' But I tell you, do not swear an oath at all: either by heaven, for it is God's throne; or by the earth, for it is his footstool; or by Jerusalem, for it is the city of the Great King. And do not swear by your head, for you cannot make even one hair white or black. All you need to say is simply 'Yes' or 'No'; anything beyond this comes from the evil one."

"What do you think that has to do with the 'Cross my heart and hope to die' thing?"

Robert raised his hand and said, "It means we shouldn't make promises we don't keep."

"That is a good answer, Robert, and I think you got most of it right. What I think Jesus is saying is that if we are going to follow him, we should never need to swear an oath or make a vow because we would always keep our promise whether we had made a vow or not. And if someone asked us a question we should simply say 'Yes' or 'No.' We wouldn't beat around the bush or hedge our bets but always be honest."

Garret raised his hand and asked, "What does 'hedge our bets' mean?"

"Oh," Fil stammered. "That's a good question. It means you won't try to say both 'Yes' and 'No' at the same time while trying to avoid giving a straight answer. So . . . that's why we don't need to say 'Cross my heart and hope to die' any more. And if you want to keep this place a secret all you have to say is, 'Yes, I'll keep it a secret.' . . . And no 'pinkie swear,' either!"

The boys laughed when Fil said 'pinkie swear' because they didn't know anyone their age that still did that anyway.

After the laughter stopped, Fil pulled some things out of his canvas bag and said they were going to make laminated bookmarks to use in their Bibles. LaShaun wrote the words of John 3:16 on his bookmark. "For God so loved the world that He gave His only Son." He was going to write the rest of the verse but he ran out of room. For lamination he covered the bookmark with two pieces of clear packing tape. The pieces of tape faced each other with the bookmark in between. LaShaun trimmed the tape close to the bookmark with a pair of scissors. He thought it turned out pretty well except for some sand that got stuck inside the tape and made it feel lumpy.

Chapter Seven
A Special Moment
Tuesday Evening

Dinner was a choice of hamburgers or hot dogs and a salad. LaShaun asked if he could have a hamburger *and* a hot dog and the lady said he could so he did. He sat with Mo, Phil and Colin again and everyone talked about what they did during free time except for LaShaun

As LaShaun carried his tray back to the clean-up area Marcy came up to him and said, "Hi! How did your afternoon go?"

LaShaun didn't realize it, but he was still smiling and he still felt so happy from his talk with Fil that he immediately said what most twelve-year-old boys would say, "All right, I guess."

Like most twelve-year-old girls Marcy could see the smile and knew exactly what LaShaun meant.

LaShaun started to say, "Thanks for asking," but somehow that didn't sound like what he wanted to say.

Marcy stood there holding her tray and she looked like she wanted to say something else, too. Instead she just smiled back at LaShaun, put her tray down and said, "I'll see you later."

LaShaun walked outside by himself and threw pinecones at the trees as though he was throwing baseballs to first base. He hit the trees almost every time. But he still didn't feel completely good about himself and he still wasn't sure where he fit in with everybody else.

When the camp bell rang, he walked down to the campfire circle and sat down next to Mo.

Worthy said, "Hey, everybody. I hope you all had fun today learning about God and Jesus! How about it, did you have fun today?"

All of the kids shouted "Yes!" Even the ones who hadn't had much fun at all. Most of LaShaun's smile had worn off but he yelled "Yes" along with everyone else and actually meant most of it.

After singing some songs, a young man LaShaun had seen down at the beach stood up and said, "Hi, my name is Ralph and I mow the grass and do stuff around the camp. Some of you already know I'm the guy that teaches the Kayak and Water Safety class.

"I really like being at camp. When I was little, I went to church camp every summer . . . not this camp but a camp just north of San Francisco."

LaShaun, who lived just north of San Francisco, wondered if the camp was somewhere near his house.

Ralph continued, "I remember one summer when I was thirteen years old. It was at the campfire on the last night of summer camp. The Camp Counselor asked everyone to think about whether they had made up their minds as to whether they wanted to follow Jesus.

"She said that Jesus was Lord and Savior whether we said he was or not. But then she said that he would never be our *own* personal Lord and Savior until we opened the door to our heart and let him in. She read these words from Revelation 3:20, 'Behold, I stand at the door and knock. If anyone hears my voice and opens the door, I will come in and eat with them and they with me.'

"I was feeling very alone at camp that year. I hadn't even sat with anybody for meals. When she read how Jesus would come in and eat with me that really meant a lot. It meant I would never have to be alone again, and that Jesus would not only be my Lord

74

and Savior but he would be my friend and my companion, too.

"The counselor asked us to bow our heads and close our eyes and then asked us to raise our hand if we wanted to ask Jesus into our hearts as Lord and Savior. My hand went up before she even finished asking the question. In all the years I had been going to camp I had never raised my hand before. It was the very first time. Then she asked everyone who had raised their hand to come down next to the fire so she could pray for us. I walked down with about twenty other kids and she prayed for us. I don't remember what she prayed about. I just remember I was surprised that I didn't feel afraid or nervous about coming down in front of everyone."

Ralph had been standing next to the fire but now he walked to the front with the fire behind his back and his face hidden in shadow.

"It was sort of like this: when I went down, I went down by myself but when I came back to my seat Jesus came with me. And he has been with me every day since. Back then, I could never have stood up in front of you and said these things. I would have been too self-conscious and embarrassed. But God has changed me. I feel so much better about myself and, when I see someone eating by themselves, I usually go over and sit with them so they don't have to feel alone like I did.

"I guess what I'm trying to say is that on Friday night you will be asked whether you want to open your heart and let Jesus in as your Lord and Savior. I hope you will say, 'Yes.'

"I did, and it was the best decision I have ever made."

Ralph stood there for a moment looking around at the faces lit up by the light of the fire. Then he turned towards Worthy and gave a little nod to say he was done and walked off into the darkness and out of sight.

Worthy said, "Let's have a prayer: Jesus, thank you for loving Ralph so much and for changing his life. I know you can do the same for each person here tonight. Lord, I pray that everyone who has not yet chosen you as their Lord and Savior will do that this week. Because that is why you came . . . so we might have your love, your forgiveness and eternal life with you. Amen."

Everyone sang one last song and then it was over.

After the campfire, all the counselors got their cabin groups together and announced that instead of going to bed they were going to take a nighttime hike up to the cross on the hill. The kids all got excited about it and the groups got all mixed up right away and friends met up with each other and kids who were from the same church formed their own groups. LaShaun and Mo stayed together and as everyone was walking up the hill kids were shining their flashlights at the trees and in each other's eyes. Kids were tripping and falling and laughing all over the place. Sometimes one kid would hide behind a tree and then jump out and say "Boo!" There were shrieks and screams and everybody had a great time.

When they got to the top LaShaun saw Marcy standing with two other girls so he went over and said, "Hi. This is my friend Mo."

Marcy turned to the two girls and said, "This is LaShaun." And then she said to LaShaun, "These are my friends, Millie and Corinne. We're from the same cabin."

After that LaShaun didn't know what to say.

Mo didn't know what to say either but he saw Colin and Phil standing over by the cross and said, "I'm going over there. Nice to meet you."

Millie and Corinne sort of disappeared and so Marcy and LaShaun were left by themselves.

Without saying anything, they both turned and walked over to the other side of the cross. This was the place where they had seen the high mountains off in the distance when they had been there during the day. But at night, instead of seeing the mountains all they saw was an uneven black place on the horizon where the stars were blocked out. There was no moon and this made the stars shine more brightly. They stood there silently, side by side, knowing that this was a special moment but not really knowing why they felt that way.

One of the counselors said, "Time to go back down." Mo came over and Marcy paused as if she was trying to decide whether to go down the hill with them or not. But Corinne and Millie grabbed her from behind and said, "Boo!" and everyone laughed when Marcy gave out a little shriek before disappearing into the dark with her friends.

Back at the cabin, Fil had the boys write the usual things in their journals. LaShaun wrote that he thought he might have seen God when he was talking to Fil that afternoon and that maybe he saw God when Ralph was talking at the campfire. He thought that maybe he saw God in some of the things the juggler had said and that maybe he saw God in the stars he saw when he was with Marcy up at the cross. It seemed to LaShaun as if God had shown up a lot that day. Or just maybe it wasn't that God had started showing up, but that LaShaun had started to pay more attention.

"Time for lights out," Fil said. And as he counted down from ten to "blast off" the boys put their journals and pencils away and snuggled themselves into a more comfortable position on their beds.

As the lights went out Robert said, "Story time!" and Phil said, "LaShaun, it's your turn to tell a story."

Fil said, "Well, LaShaun, do you want to tell a story tonight? It doesn't have to be a long one . . . well?"

For some reason he couldn't quite understand LaShaun felt as though it might be the right thing for him to tell another story. Just like on Monday, he had no idea what the story might turn out to be but he had a funny feeling that if there was a story to be told, God would take care of it.

"Okay," he heard himself say. "Here's a story:"

"Once there was a man who wanted to know his next-door neighbor better. So, he fixed dinner, carried it over to his neighbor's house and knocked on the door. He hoped that maybe they could eat it together.

"But no one answered the door, even though it was obvious that someone was there. He could see where the curtains had been pulled open ever so slightly, as if someone was trying to look through them without being seen. Yet in spite of this, no one came to open the door.

"The man was very disappointed but the food was still warm and ready to be eaten. So, he went to another neighbor's house, and knocked on the door.

"This time the door was opened and the man was invited in. The food was shared, and the two of them became friends. When he left, his new friend showed him where he kept the key to this house hidden in a potted plant.

"'You don't have to knock anymore,' he said. 'You can consider the house to be your own.'

"The next day, the man brought more food to the first neighbor's house. Once again, he knocked, and again no one opened the door.

"'Open up,' he shouted. 'I've got food for dinner and I thought that we could eat it together.'

"But the door stayed shut and locked. So once again, he carried the food to another house and shared the food with someone else.

"The man was so eager to be friends with the neighbor next door that he returned, day after day, and each time he brought food to share.

"One day the neighbor died. Until the very end, he kept himself locked up with his own family and friends. He never got to know his neighbor and he never tasted how good the food was—food that had been cooked especially for him.

"Even today the man with the food goes out looking for new friends. Whenever he comes to a house, he knocks on the door, always hoping someone will invite him to come in."

LaShaun stopped; for the story had come to an end and he had nothing else to say.

The story puzzled him a great deal because he didn't know where the words had come from. He had used words he had never used or even known before. Later, when he thought about it, he realized the story was not as original as he had thought. It was really just the same story Ralph had told at the campfire earlier that evening.

Fil and the other boys could tell that, too. They knew right away the man was Jesus. But there was something about the way LaShaun told the story that made them wonder if Jesus was, in fact, knocking at their door and, if they heard it, whether they would ignore it or open it up and invite him in.

Fil said, "That story is probably more than enough for tonight. I'm going to think about it some more before I fall asleep. I hope you all will, too. Good night."

Some of the boys said "Good night" back at him, and LaShaun fell asleep wondering along with the others if Jesus was knocking at his door, and if he was, whether he would open it for him or not.

Chapter Eight
The Power of the Wind
Wednesday Morning

Once again, the day began with devotions. Fil told the boys to draw a picture of a hungry person knocking on the door to their house; someone who didn't have any food or anything else to share.

"This is sort of like the story you heard last night but also sort of different. I want you to write down what you would do if you lived in that house."

When they had all stopped writing, Fil read from Matthew 25:

"And Jesus said, I was a stranger and you did not welcome me, naked and you did not give me clothing, sick and in prison and you did not visit me. Then they also will answer, 'Lord, when was it that we saw you hungry or thirsty or a stranger or naked or sick or in prison, and did not take care of you?' Then he will answer them, 'Truly I tell you, just as you did not do it to one of the least of these, you did not do it to me.'

Now I want you to think what Jesus would do if he lived in your house

This made most of the boys feel very uncomfortable because they had thought of so many good reasons why they should not answer the door or let the man in. Like most people, however, they didn't think about it for very long. After all, they were getting ready for breakfast and, when the camp bell rang, they left the cabin in a hurry.

After breakfast, the four boys' cabin groups were told to follow their counselors across the camp to the small chapel that stood between the Director's house and the girls' cabins.

Inside the chapel, they saw that the blinds had been pulled down over the windows. After they sat, a man stood up and said he was a missionary serving in a small city of 150,000 people in central Nigeria. He taught English to children at a Christian school and used the Bible as the textbook.

"Nigeria," he said, "is in West Africa and is usually a safe and peaceful place to live. Some years ago, people in the northern part of the country started fighting against the Christians who lived there. Many Christians were attacked, some of them were killed and their houses and churches were burned down. At first, they tried to be like Jesus and refused to fight back. Later, some of them did fight back. This got more people involved in the fighting."

All of this made LaShaun feel very uncomfortable. He liked happy stories more than stories like this one.

The man went on, "Since then things have gotten worse and the city where I serve is sort of caught in the middle of it all. Some of the people whose homes had burned moved onto the grounds of the Christian School. By the time I left to come back to the United States for a year off, the school grounds had become nearly covered with tents. There is barely enough food to feed everyone who needs it.

"So," he said, "I decided to spend the year travelling around telling people about the situation at the school and asking for people to support the ministry. Twenty-five percent of the financial support will be used to buy food for the people who are living at the school and the rest will make it possible for me to go back and be with the children again."

While he was talking, he was showing pictures of the city where he lived, pictures of some of the houses and churches that had been burned, and a lot of pictures showing children playing, studying, worshiping and always smiling. There were also pictures of sad-looking women who, even though they were sad because they had lost their homes, were still wearing beautiful, loose-fitting clothing covered with the most beautiful colors and patterns LaShaun had ever seen. He felt so bad about what the man had said that he reached into his pocket where he kept a few dollars "just in case."

He wanted to be ready to give it away when the offering plate was passed around.

But it turned out there wasn't going to be an offering because, as the man put it, "It wouldn't be right to ask children for money."

LaShaun didn't see anything wrong with it but didn't say anything . . . except for joining with everyone else in saying "Amen" when the missionary finished up his final prayer.

After the missionary's talk, the kids were invited up to the front of the chapel so they could touch and feel some of the small carvings, crayon pictures and beaded jewelry that had been made by the school children in Nigeria. These were also on sale but the man said he wasn't going to sell any of them while he was at the camp. He did give every child one of his business cards with his name, phone number, mailing address, email address and the address to his personal website. If they really wanted to buy something, they could find out about it on his website and then ask their parents if they would be willing to buy it for them. As they left the chapel, they noticed the man and some of the camp staff were already starting to put up the window blinds to let the sunlight back in.

After their morning snacks the four boys' groups split up and headed off in different directions while the girls' groups headed towards the chapel. The Elijah group followed Fil back to the secret place they had discovered the day before.

After everyone had sat down at one of the two picnic tables Fil said, "Here is something we can make this morning."

He reached into the bag he was carrying and pulled out a bunch of copier paper, two rolls of tape, a box of straws an eight pairs of children's safety scissors and a box of paper clips. After dividing them up between the two tables he reached into the bag again and pulled out a small pinwheel attached to a straw. He held it up and blew on it and the pinwheel spun around and around faster and faster.

"Here is how you are going to make your pinwheel."

He un-bent the paperclip that held his pinwheel to the straw and the pinwheel all unfolded into a sort of strange, bent and twisted star shape.

"Here is a pencil. Now push my pinwheel flat on your paper and trace around it with the pencil. Then pass them over to the next person. Then take the scissors and cut out the shape along the pencil lines. When you have done that—and do it very carefully—raise your hand and I will show you how to do the rest."

It didn't take long for the first boy to raise his hand. Fil showed him how to fold the points of the star into the middle of the design and how to tape them down with the tape. Then he showed them how to poke a hole through the center of the paper and then through the straw. Then all they had to do was to stick the paperclip through both holes and bend it in a certain way. And then they had a pinwheel to blow on.

LaShaun's pinwheel looked bent out of shape and it didn't spin around when he blew on it. So, Fil showed him how to fix it so it would spin. He had to do this with several of the boys and before they knew it, they were spinning all over the place.

Fil said that Jesus compared the Holy Spirit with the wind. They both are invisible but they both come with power. Just as the wind makes your pinwheel spin, the Holy Spirit can help you to do things you could never do without its power.

"Like Jesus healing someone!" one boy shouted.

"Or like praying for something and it comes true!" said another.

They all shouted out examples. Some of them didn't seem quite right to Fil but he didn't say anything. He figured the boys would eventually figure it out for themselves . . . if, of course, they kept following Jesus.

It was getting close to lunch time so Fil gave a short prayer, the camp bell rang and the younger boys ran down the hill as fast as they could go, holding their pinwheels up high so they would spin in the air.

Chapter Nine
Maybe Tomorrow
Wednesday Afternoon

Lunch was grilled cheese sandwiches with celery and carrot sticks. LaShaun kept his pinwheel in a safe place where it wouldn't get smushed. As he ate his sandwich, he couldn't wait to show the pinwheel to Marcy. Then the thought came to him that her group might have made pinwheels today, too. As it turned out, everyone in the camp had made pinwheels that morning and, as soon as lunch was over all the kids ran outside to see whose pinwheel spun around the fastest.

Marcy and LaShaun blew on each other's pinwheel and laughed when LaShaun's paper clip fell out and his pinwheel went spinning away like a Frisbee! But when the bell rang, they had to hurry back to their cabins to get ready for their swimming class.

At the swimming pool, they started out by playing "Ping Pong Ruckus." The kids were divided into two teams who stood in the water on opposite sides of the shallow end of the pool. Each team had a large bucket on the edge of the pool. At the count of three the teacher dumped a huge box of ping pong balls into the middle of the pool. The team that put the most balls into their bucket was the winner. There was lots of splashing and grabbing and LaShaun figured that no one could have swum through the mess even if they knew how.

After the game, they practiced their back floats again. The teacher then had them roll over onto their stomachs and kick their legs as they held on to the edge of the pool. Once again, the water flew all over the place. LaShaun kicked so hard and his legs got so tired that he couldn't kick any more. Before the class ended the teacher had each kid try kicking their legs while they floated on their backs. Most of the kids actually moved around in the water when they did this but none of them went in a straight line.

After swimming LaShaun went up to Marcy and asked if they were still going to spend free time together.

"I'd like to," she said with a sigh, "but . . . you know how you couldn't yesterday? Well . . . I can't today because Kelli, one of the girls in my cabin . . . it's her birthday today and her Mom brought up all these cookies and stuff on Sunday and had them kept in the camp kitchen so that our cabin could have a party for her today. So, I have to go."

"That's not fair," said LaShaun. "I mean we only get five 'free times' all week. I think it's selfish to make you all give it up for someone's birthday party."

Marcy started moving her hands and arms as if she wanted to do something with them but she didn't.

Instead, she said, "I've got to go. Maybe tomorrow for sure!" and she was gone.

LaShaun spent "Free Time" doing what he had done on Monday: He just sort of wandered around the camp with his hands in his pockets watching the other kids having a good time. But as he walked, he wondered if he would ever tell another story like the ones he had already told. The more he thought about it the more he wondered how it would happen. Would he make the story up himself or would God just sort of give him one to tell like the last two times? As he walked around the camp, he tried to think up a good story but even though he tried and tried, he couldn't come up with a single idea for one.

After the free time was over LaShaun wandered back to his cabin. All the Elijah boys were really tired from the swimming and running they had been doing so Fil just had them lie down on the grass and look up at the sky like he had done on Monday night.

"What do you see?" he asked.

One of the bigger boys said, "I see clouds. I see a big, dark one over there."

One of the other boys said, "I see the trees pointing up. They look really tall from down here."

LaShaun said he saw where a jet plane had flown across the sky and the other boys saw things like a bird, or the sun, and one even said he could see the wind! LaShaun looked as hard as he could but he didn't think he saw the wind anywhere. He could feel it, he could see the clouds moving and the tree branches blowing around but the wind was invisible to him.

After everyone had shared what they saw Fil pulled out the little Bible from his back pocket and turned the pages until he found what he was looking for.

"Here's something from Psalm 147:

> Sing to the LORD with grateful praise;
>   make music to our God on the harp.
> He covers the sky with clouds;
>   he supplies the earth with rain
>   and makes grass grow on the hills

After reading this he closed his Bible and put it back in his pocket.

Then he said, "On Monday night we listened to what the stars were telling us. The Bible told us they were telling us about how amazing God is. The Bible tells us the clouds and the sky and just about everything else are telling us something about God, too.

"Palm 147 tells us that we should sing songs, play music and praise the Lord for everything God has made. I want you to know that if you want to find out more about God all you have to do is look around you. You can look up or you can look down or you can look in any direction you want. No matter where you look you will find something that will tell you something about God. The world is full of stories just waiting for you to slow down and listen to them. And most of the stories you hear will be about God. That is if you are really listening and really wanting to hear.

"That's enough. Take a break before dinner and we'll do a craft or two, tomorrow afternoon."

Most of the boys went back to the cabin and sat or lay down on their bunks. Some of them read and some of them fell asleep, but not for very long. Soon the camp bell rang again letting everyone know that dinner was ready.

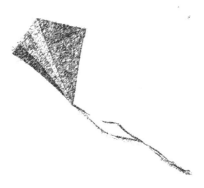

Chapter Ten
Ka-Boom
Wednesday Evening

Dinner was chili on toast with salad and fruit. LaShaun didn't really like chili very much but there were pieces of hot dogs in it so he picked them out. He was still hungry so he scraped the chili off to the side and ate what was left of the soggy toast.

Just before dinner was over LaShaun heard a loud noise like a chair falling over from the other side of the Dining Hall. Some boys started yelling and someone threw their glass of juice into someone's face. Two of the boys from the Moses cabin started hitting each other with their fists. A few of the other kids stood around and yelled at them to hit each other harder. Fil and two of the other counselors ran over and grabbed the two boys and pulled them away from each other. They told the other kids to back off and had the two boys sit down and wait until the camp director and Worthy got there.

The director said something to the two boys. Then, along with Worthy and the boys' cabin counselor, they all walked out of the Dining Hall and over to the camp office. For a long time, everyone was talking about the fight but, after a while, everyone got sort of tired about it and went back to whatever they had been talking about earlier.

Later, LaShaun heard that the director had called the boy's parents and they had to drive all the way up to the camp that night and take them home. LaShaun felt sorry for the boys and their parents and wondered why the director didn't give them a second chance to stay at the camp. He figured that maybe the director knew more about it than he did so he stopped wondering about it.

All during dinner, LaShaun had been looking around the room for Marcy but he couldn't see where she was sitting. As he was getting up to clear off his tray, he felt a tap on the back of his shoulder. It was Marcy.

"Where were you? LaShaun asked. "I was looking all over for you."

"I was right behind you the whole time," she said. "You were looking for me everyplace but right next to you!"

"Well . . ." LaShaun paused, as though he wasn't sure he should finish the sentence or not. He decided to finish it and said, "I was thinking we could have had dinner together."

"I was thinking the same thing," she said. "Maybe we could. . . you know . . . do you mind if I sat with you at the campfire tonight?"

LaShaun started to smile but realized he already was.

So, he let the smile alone and said, "Sure."

He wanted to add, "I'd like that," but he didn't.

It was starting to feel chilly outside and the wind was starting to pick up. LaShaun said he needed to get his jacket from his cabin so they walked there first. As they walked LaShaun wondered if this was sort of like going out on a date. He wondered if they should be holding hands and whether he was supposed to kiss her later when they said good-night after the campfire.

He knew this wasn't really a date and he knew he didn't have to do those things but he did wonder what it would be like . . . and he enjoyed wondering about it. He wondered about it so much that he completely forgot about Marcy, and after he got his jacket from the cabin, he started walking to the campfire without her.

"Hey! Wait up!" she shouted.

LaShaun felt embarrassed.

He started to feel like a failure again but he remembered what he had learned from the juggler and from Fil . . . that he didn't need to feel like a failure anymore . . . and the feeling immediately went away.

"Oops," is what he said. "Sorry!"

He waited for her to catch up and he really did feel like holding her hand. He had never felt this way about a girl before and he wondered whether she was feeling the same way about him. There was no way he could have known it, of course, but she was.

As they waited for the evening campfire program to start LaShaun said this was the first time he had ever been to a summer camp and that he really liked it. He asked if Marcy had ever been to camp before.

"Yes," she said. "I have. In fact, this is the second time I've been to a camp this summer."

"To this camp?" LaShaun asked.

"No, not here," she said. "Right after school let out, I went to camp back in Ohio. That's where I live. I'm just spending the month with my grandparents in Yuba City and they signed me up to come here as part of my visit."

LaShaun felt very disappointed to learn that Marcy lived so far away. Somehow, he hoped they would be able to see each other after the week at camp was over. It didn't make any sense that they would but . . . well . . . that just the way he felt about it.

Marcy seemed to know what he was thinking so she said, "I don't know. Maybe I'll come back next summer. It would be fun if I . . . we . . . if we both were at camp . . . at the same time . . . again."

LaShaun said, "Me too," just as Worthy stood up with her guitar and said, "Let's praise God with a song."

So, everyone sang a song and then another song. Then the counselor from the King David cabin stood up and opened his Bible. He held the Bible in one hand and held a flashlight with the other so he could read the words.

"I have come," he read, "so that you might have life. And that you might have it to the full."

Then he put the Bible down and said he was having a great time at camp this week. He was busy doing something every minute and it was all good. Every day was filled with games and crafts and worship and study and good food and he had made so many new friends. Just like Jesus said, my life is full!"

"But," he continued, "I don't think this is exactly what Jesus was talking about. You see I don't really need Jesus to have a week like this. I could be doing this somewhere else that wasn't a Christian camp. I could be at a Boy Scout camp and still feel my life was full.

"This is what I think . . . I think Jesus was talking about something different . . . something more than this. You see, after this week is over and after we have all gone home, everything that has been fun at camp and most of the friends we have made and the counselors and the swimming in the lake and all of that will be gone. We'll feel empty inside, as though something is missing. Jesus didn't come so we would be full and then be empty again. He came so we might be full of life all the time!"

The campfire suddenly exploded in a shower of sparks and embers. Some of them reached all the way to a group of girls sitting on the front bench. The girls screamed and waved their hands around to brush it off of their clothes.

Most of the other kids started laughing but Worthy stood up and told them that it would be better to pray for the girls than to laugh at them.

"Would Jesus laugh at them?" She asked.

Everybody knew that Worthy was right and the kids down near the front went over, said they were sorry, and hoped that the girls were all right.

When everything had settled down, the King David leader continued his talk.

"What Jesus means is that if we let him into our lives and let him live in us all the time then he will be the one who will fill our hearts and minds with good things. When we know that we are never alone—when we know that we are always being loved—then we know that if we walk with Jesus, we will never really need to worry about doing what everyone else is doing. We will never need to worry whether we look good enough, or whether we are smart enough, or popular enough. We'll never have to worry about those things ever again. Because Jesus has filled us with joy and hope and a peace that is better than all of those things put together. "

LaShaun didn't understand everything that the man was saying. But he knew that some of it had to do with being happier with Jesus than without him. But he also knew that even with Jesus his family was not happy all of the time.

Maybe, he wondered, *it would be even worse if we didn't have Jesus.*

"If we take Jesus home with us from camp, we will never need to feel empty again . . . "

Everyone could tell he was about to finish up his devotional talk but he never did.

Suddenly the sky lit up as if God had taken a flash photo of the whole world. The light was immediately followed by a crash, and a boom that almost knocked everyone off the benches. The sound echoed back and forth from every hill and mountain. Then, as if that was not enough, it started to hail. At first there were just a few pieces of hail. Some of the kids were frightened but most were excited and some of them picked up the hail and popped it in their mouths. But that didn't last very long because suddenly the hail started falling so hard and so thick that everyone pulled their jackets over their heads and started running back to their cabins.

The ground quickly became covered with so much hail that it looked as if it had snowed. Then, just as suddenly as it had started, the hail stopped. There was silence for a few seconds followed by another bright flash and another "ka-boom!" Without saying a word, LaShaun and Marcy headed off in opposite directions and, while he ran, LaShaun wondered if this was like the sound the keg of dynamite made when Bent-Pan Billy stuck his pick into it.

Now, instead of the hail, it began to rain. Huge drops of rain splattered on the ground. At first, like the hail, the raindrops fell one at a time. Then they began to fall faster and harder. LaShaun ran into the cabin just as the entire camp was filled with the sound of water pouring down. It sounded as if they had suddenly fallen into the center of a massive waterfall with the roof of the cabin beating like a giant drum.

In spite of the downpour, LaShaun breathed in the air. It smelled so fresh and new it seemed as though God was starting to create the world all over again.

The little black cloud that one of the boys had seen before dinner now must have filled the whole sky. Some of the kids started thinking about Noah and the ark, and the camp counselors and staff started thinking about all the windows they needed to close and what they needed to do to get everybody calmed down and ready for bed.

Earlier that afternoon when Fil read that, "God supplies the earth with rain," he probably hadn't been thinking about this!

Back in the Elijah cabin Fil did a head count and found that all eight boys were there. He told them to get out of their wet clothes and get ready for bed.

One of the boys said, "But I haven't brushed my teeth yet!"

And Fil said, "If you want to run out to the bathroom in all this rain to brush your teeth be my guest!"

Then it dawned on him that everyone probably needed to go to the bathroom for other reasons . . . including himself, so he said, "Forget about getting ready for bed. Let's all make a run for it now so we don't have to do it later! Our clothes are already wet so who cares!"

They all ran through rain and the across the wet, sandy ground to the bathrooms and back, laughing and shouting as if it was the most fun they'd had all week—until the sky started lighting up like fireworks, with one flash of lightning after another. The sound of the thunder was deafening and Fil realized there was a real danger someone could get hurt. He was glad when everyone got back to the cabin in one piece.

"Now," he said, "we can get ready for bed."

After everyone had changed and climbed into their bunks Fil said, "Okay, get out your journals and write something about what you saw and heard and thought about today. And remember to write down where you saw God."

Most of the boys started writing. LaShaun wrote that he saw God in the lightning and thunder. He wrote about his talk with Fil and what the juggler said about not being a failure the day before. Then he started to write something about Marcy but was worried his father or one of the other boys might read his journal and he wouldn't want them to know about that.

So he just wrote, "It was a good day and I smiled a lot."

It was still earlier than the other nights when they usually turned off the lights so Fil left the lights on and said, "Hey, I almost forgot. Did any of you have a story to tell about the rock you found on Monday afternoon? Here's your chance. You've got a captive audience!"

Garret, who was the smallest boy in the cabin, raised his hand and said, "I have a story."

Fill said, "Let's hear it. But talk loud enough for us to hear with all this rain coming down on the roof."

Here is the story he told:

"I can't show you my rock because I don't have it anymore. My rock was a thin, flat one like the ones you can skip on the water. I thought it looked a little like a flying saucer but I couldn't figure out what that would have to do with Jesus . . . I mean I couldn't figure out what Jesus would say if he was going to tell a story about it. So, I thought that one day when Jesus was alive a flying saucer landed next to the Sea of Galilee and three little men came out of it. They each had two heads and green squiggly things instead of hair. Otherwise they looked normal.

"They asked the first people they saw to 'Take us to your leader.'

"One person said he would take them to the king. Another said he would take them to the mayor and another one said he would take them all the way to

Rome so they could meet the Caesar. The space men didn't know which one to choose so they just stood there for a long time talking about it.

"Then Peter, the disciple, walked up and said, 'I'll take you to Jesus.' They thought that was a good idea so they walked with Peter over to where Jesus was.

"When Jesus saw the space men, he treated them like he did everybody else. He told them that he loved them and that he would forgive all their sins and that when he died on the cross, he would be dying for them, too.

"This made the space men very happy so they said, 'Good-bye,' and went back to their space ship and took off. And that's the end of the story."

Fil started clapping and a few of the other boys clapped along with him just to be polite.

Then Fil said, "That was a good story. I think it reminds us that Jesus really does love everybody in the whole universe and beyond!

"Now," he added, "Does anyone else have a story to tell?"

Nobody raised their hands but one of the boys said, "Now it's your turn, Fil. Tell us one of your stories."

Fil looked at LaShaun as though asking him if he wanted to tell another story.

LaShaun knew what Fil was doing but he just shook his head, "No."

So, Fil said, "I'll tell a story, but first I'm going to turn the lights off."

Before he could reach for the switch there was another flash of lightning, a crash of thunder and the lights all went out by themselves.

Fil flipped the light switch back and forth a few times and said, "That was perfect timing, wasn't it? Well, I might as well just go ahead and tell the story.

"There was a boy. He had a name but it doesn't matter what it was. At least not as far as this story is concerned. Actually, there are a lot of things about this boy that are very interesting but I am just going to skip over them so I can get straight to the good part.

"The boy lived next to the ocean where the wind blew soft and steady most of the time. Once in a while the wind didn't blow at all and sometimes it blew so hard that it knocked trees down. But mostly there was a gentle breeze that was perfect for flying a kite. And flying kites is what this boy liked to do more than anything else.

"It didn't matter what sort of kite it was, either. He flew big kites and tiny kites, box kites and kites in the shape of birds and animals. Some of his kites were long tubes with fringes that made them look like dragons or sea creatures. Some were so large his father had to help him get them into the air and then tie them to the back of the car because they pulled so hard.

"The best place to fly the kites was on the beach where there were no trees or electrical wires. Looking up at the kites made him look at the sky which made him think of heaven. And thinking about heaven made him think about God and thinking about God made him think about prayer. As a result, whenever the boy went down to the beach and flew his kites he talked to God.

"Sometimes he told God what was going on in school or what he was doing with his friends. He talked to God about his family and shared his hopes and dreams. Sometimes he got angry at God for sad things that would happen but mostly he was a happy boy who would tell God jokes and laugh at them himself.

"Occasionally he would spend the whole day looking up at his kite and asking God questions about why things were the way they were, or where things came from. At other times he would ask God to do things for him. He would ask God to make a sick relative well. He would ask God to help his friend's parents stay together. He would ask to do well in school and he would ask God to help everyone in his own family get along with each other.

"More than anything else, he wanted to know about God. He wanted to know God like he knew his friends.

"So, as he flew his kites. he would stare hard at the sky and wonder where God lived. He wondered if God was peeking down at him from behind a cloud or whether God was shining in the sun, touching him with the wind or talking to him with the roar of the ocean waves. Even at night when he wasn't flying a kite he would look up at the heavens and wonder if the twinkling of the stars was God winking at him, or whether the face he saw on the moon was the face of God looking down at him.

"'Where are you, God?' he would ask.

"Sometimes he would shout the words as loud as he could just in case it would help God hear him better. But God never showed up or said anything to him. It was as though God didn't hear his questions or was simply ignoring them.

"After a time, the boy began to think that maybe God wasn't real at all. Maybe everything about God was just made up. So, the boy stopped talking to God and began to think about other things while he was flying his kites.

"After many years the boy grew up and moved away. He stopped flying kites and stopped thinking about God.

"He thought he was happy but he wasn't. Not really. He wasn't even close to being as happy as he had been when he had been a boy, talking to God as flew his kites on the beach.

"Many years later when he was an old man, he was lying in bed thinking about his life. For some reason he started talking to God again. He didn't mean to, but it just sort of happened.

"'Come on, God. Why didn't you ever answer my prayer? I looked for you everywhere and you never showed up!'

"And then, for the first time in his life, the man heard God speak. God spoke in a very quiet voice directly to the man's heart and mind without bothering to go through his ears. The voice just simply *was*, as though God was not far away in the sky at all, but right there with him in the room or maybe even closer to him than that. What he heard God say was this:

"'My dear child, you say you looked for me everywhere. But you didn't. You were too busy flying your kites and so you kept your eyes up in the sky all the time. You thought you would find me up there. I was up there, of course, but that was not where I wanted to spend time with you. I didn't want to be with you from so far away. So, I came down to be close to you. But you never looked for me there.

109

"'I sent you a book so you could learn more about me. I put the book right there in your house. In fact, your parents gave you the book the very day you asked me to show myself to you. But you never read the book. It sat on the shelf in your room and, when you grew up and moved away you did not take it with you.

"'If you had read the book you would have learned how I had actually come down to be in the world. I came so everyone who wanted to know me would be able to find me. I came as a person whose name was Jesus. I loved you so much that I wanted to be as close to you as possible and I wanted you to know me as well as you knew your best friend.

"'Your whole life I have been with you, hoping you would find me. But you have spent your life looking up and around at the stars and the clouds, and searching for me in the words and thoughts of other people. You imagined what I was like and pretended that what you imagined was who I really was.

"'But you were wrong. I am not the creation of your imagination. I am who I am. And finally, today, you looked for me in your heart instead of somewhere else. And you found me.

"'Yet you will never meet me face to face until you look into the face of Jesus. That is how I came into the world and that is still the way I reveal myself to people today.'

"The man never heard the voice of God that way again. But he did begin to read about Jesus in the Bible and he slowly began to learn about the God he had once imagined but had never really known. He learned that God was greater than the heavens but as close to him as the wind is to a kite. And he learned that God held him up in much that same way

"When the man grew even older, he died. He found himself in heaven with more kites to fly than he could count. The kites were more beautiful than any he had owned when he was a boy and they flew on the winds of eternity with a wondrous grace that brought tears of joy to his heart.

"And the One who made the heavens and the earth . . . the One who made the wind to blow, the waves to roar, and the stars to shine . . . stood next to him and shared his joy. And that, as it turned out, was the most wonderful thing of all."

There was silence in the cabin until Fil said, "Now, if you are not already asleep, go to sleep."

As the boys fell asleep in the darkness, the sound of the rain became the sound of the wind on a kite. And the boys soared through the sky in their dreams.

Chapter Eleven
Tricks
Thursday Morning

When the boys woke up in the morning, they discovered that Fil had posted a sign on the cabin door. The words on the sign said. "No Jesus, No God . . . Know Jesus, Know God."

During their devotions, Fil had one of the boys read a verse from the Bible that said, "He who has seen me has seen the Father. For I and the Father are one."

Fil asked if anyone had any idea what Jesus was talking about when he said this.

No one raised their hands or said anything so Fil asked the question again.

"Well? You heard this verse at the campfire on Monday night. So, any ideas?"

Colin raised his hand and said, "I think it is the same thing you wrote on the sign that's hanging on the door."

Fil quietly said, "I think you're right," and told everyone to get ready for breakfast.

But first, LaShaun opened up his journal and wrote down, "No Jesus, No God . . . Know Jesus, Know God."

Then, after thinking about it, he added the word, "kite" and then, "look for God next to you in Jesus."

As he got dressed and brushed his teeth, he began to feel a story forming somewhere deep inside. He didn't know what it was but he knew it was there. And he knew that sometime soon it was going to come out. He felt a little nervous about it but also a little excited. After all, there was nothing he liked more than to listen to a good story; even his own when he heard it for the first time.

It was still raining when they left the cabin and walked towards the Dining Hall, but it wasn't raining very hard. They could even see a few places where the sun was trying to break through the gray clouds that stretched across the sky everywhere they looked.

Breakfast was oatmeal and cinnamon toast. A lot of the kids didn't like oatmeal so the cold cereal and milk were more popular than usual. As usual LaShaun sat with Mo, Phil and Colin. Two of the other boys in their cabin were already sitting at the table when they got there. They were two of the bigger boys. One of them was Marty, the boy who had told the story about the baseball that had turned into a princess before turning into a rock. The other boy was Phil's brother, Glen.

Marty and Glen shared a bunk bed and had been to camp together before. This was the third year that they had been to the camp. All week they had acted as if they knew everything about everything and treated the rest of the boys like they were little children, except for Robert, who was the same age and size that they were.

But today, for a change, they actually seemed to be nice.

"It's been a pretty good week so far, don't you think?" Marty said to Glen.

And Glen said, "Yeah. I didn't think it was going to turn out good, especially being stuck with Fil for a counselor. But Fil turned out to be pretty good, too. He doesn't yell at us or anything."

"And he tells good stories," added Colin.

"I guess," Glen replied. "But hey, LaShaun, you've told some pretty good stories, too. Do you have any other stories you can tell us? Maybe you can tell another story tonight instead of Fil?"

Just like before, LaShaun didn't know what to say. Maybe he would have a story to tell that night or maybe he wouldn't.

He figured that if he had one it would be up to God to tell it, so he said, "Maybe, I don't know."

Marty and Glen both shrugged their shoulders and went back to eating their cold cereal.

On the way out of the Dining Hall LaShaun saw Marcy across the room. This time he was the one who went over and said, "Hi."

"That was quite a storm last night, wasn't it?" he said.

"None of us slept very well in the girls' cabin," Marcy said. "It felt as though . . . well . . . it was just too dark and noisy."

"We stayed up and told stories like we do every night," LaShaun said. "It was a lot of fun."

"We don't tell stories in our cabin," Marcy said with a sad sort of look on her face. "I wish we did. Whenever we talk too much and can't go to sleep Tracy reads to us from the Bible and says a prayer to get us to quiet down. I wish she would read some of the stories in the Bible instead of just verses. I like stories, and I think God tells the best stories in the world!"

LaShaun had never thought about God like this before. He knew the Bible had stories in it and he knew Jesus liked to tell stories, too, so maybe Marcy was right.

He also remembered when Fil had said that LaShaun's stories might be a gift from God. All week he had thought Fil made up good stories. But he knew his own stories hadn't been ones he had made up. They had just shown up. Maybe that was how Fil came up with his stories, and maybe Jesus' stories came from God, too. Maybe God *was* where all the best stories in the world came from!

For a moment, just like the night before, he almost forgot he was with Marcy. When he noticed her again, she was looking at him with a funny expression on her face as if she was trying to figure out what LaShaun was thinking about.

LaShaun didn't know what to say so he just said, "Hey, I gotta go. Maybe we can . . . you know . . . get together during free time . . . is that . . . I mean . . . do you want to like we didn't do yesterday?"

He knew he was all mixed up, but Marcy smiled and said, "Sure, right after swimming."

Back at the cabin Fil got the boys together.

"Because it is still raining," he said, "all the girls are going to have the first of this morning's program in The Dining Hall. We're going to start off in the Chapel."

So off they went through the wet drizzle across the camp to the Chapel.

Instead of a missionary this time there was a woman dressed in a clown outfit with a stool, a very small tricycle and what looked like a short rope tightrope on the front platform.

After all, four of the boys' cabins had gotten settled she said, "Good morning. My name is Monica and your names are . . .?"

All the boys just sat there not knowing what to say.

So she said, "Go ahead, why don't you get it over with and all say your names at the same time. Ready?"

And then she counted out loud, "One, two, three . . . go!"

All the boys shouted out their names at the same time. Some of them shouted their names over and over and then they all started laughing.

The counselors all thought it was getting out of control so two of them started shouting, "Boys, stop it right . . . ."

But Monica interrupted them by saying, "Oh, leave them alone and let them laugh! It's a wet, gloomy day and they deserve to be having a good time."

The boys who heard her say this fell in love with her immediately. And the boys who hadn't heard what she said loved her, too, because she was smiling and laughing along with them.

After a minute or two Monica raised her hands and started talking in a quiet voice, "It's time to calm down. It's time to calm down."

Most of the boys quieted down right away and, when some of the other boys kept making noise, the quieter ones started to say, "Shhh! We can't hear what the lady is saying. Shhh!" And, to the counselors' surprise, they did.

"Now," Monica said when she got their attention, "I would like to introduce you to a friend of mine. Nicky, come on out and say 'Hello' to all these nice boys."

The small door next to her opened slightly, and a very small, silky-haired dog came running out and did a perfect back flip in front of everybody.

"Good job, Nicky!" Monica said as she tossed a small doggie treat into the air.

Nicky caught it easily and some of the boys gave Nicky a clap along with two or three loud and shrieky whistles.

"Now boys, my little friends are going to do some tricks for you but you will have to be quiet so they don't get too distracted. They need to focus their attention on me if they are going to do their tricks well."

The Chapel became so quiet that LaShaun could hear Nicky panting.

Monica then asked Nicky, "Who's your Momma?" and the pup jumped straight up and into her arms.

She turned to the boys and said, "Nicky couldn't do these things when I first met her. She was only three weeks old when I got her from an animal shelter. She is a very smart dog and learns her tricks very quickly. Most dogs do not like to be up in a high place and they don't like to jump down off of things. But Nicky isn't afraid to do that, are you my little snookums?"

In response, Nicky put her front paws on Monica's shoulders, and then jumped out of her arms, standing on her shoulders with her paws up in the air.

"Are you ready, dear?" Monica asked. "All right then . . . Nicky . . . go!"

Nicky jumped high in the air while doing another back flip and landed in the middle of a very soft beanbag pillow.

"Wasn't that a good trick?" Monica said to no one in particular. "Let's all give her a big hand!"

The boys gave her one as Nicky walked off the platform and out through the door.

"Dogs," Monica said, "do not know how to do these things when they are born, and they don't do them when they grow up, either . . . unless someone like me trains them to do the tricks."

She looked around at the boys and then said, "Have any of you learned anything at camp this week?"

A few of the boys put their hands up in the air.

"Good," she said. "You are the sort of boys that can learn to do a lot of things!"

Immediately, almost all of the other hands went up, too.

"Oh, good," Monica said. "God can use a bunch of boys like you who are ready and willing to learn new things. Now I want you to meet another friend of mine. Come on in, Mitzi, and show yourself."

In trotted a small, white poodle, complete with a small pom-pom at the end of her tail. She walked right up to Monica, jumped up onto the small stool and sat down looking out at all the boys.

"Now," Monica said, "Mitzi is a smart dog. You may find this hard to believe but Mitzi is able to talk. Would you like to hear her talk?"

All the boys shouted out "Yes!"

"Mitzi can do more than talk. She can answer questions, too. Would you like to see her answer some questions?"

Again, the boys shouted, "Yes!"

All right, Mitzi. Here is your first question. What is on the outside of a tree?"

Without missing a beat Mitzi barked once.

"Did you hear that? I asked Mitzi what is on the outside of a tree and she said, 'Bark!' Isn't that amazing?"

Most of the boys started laughing again and a few, who had been daydreaming or poking one another and weren't paying attention, just sat there, looking around the room and wondering what they missed.

"Well," Monica said. "Would you like me to ask her another question?"

"Yes!" the boys shouted.

"All right, Mitzi. Here is your second question. What is on the top of a house?"

Again, without missing a beat, Mitzi barked twice.

"Did you hear that? I asked Mitzi what is on the top of a house and she said, 'Roof! Roof!' What a smart doggie you are."

As the boys laughed, she tossed Mitzi a doggie treat.

"All right, one more question for Mitzi. Now Mitzi, pay attention because this is going to be a hard one. Who do you think was the greatest baseball player of all time?"

This time Mitzi barked three times.

"Are you sure?" Monica said.

Then she turned to the boys.

"You heard what she said. I asked her who the greatest baseball player of all time was and she said, "Ruth! Ruth! Ruth! Three times."

All the boys started laughing again as Monica said, "But I think she is wrong. I think it was Joe DiMaggio."

And the boys laughed even harder.

"Thank you, Mitzi. You did a wonderful job answering all those questions. You can go back to your room now."

And Mitzi trotted back through the door.

"You see," said Monica, "There are two types of people in the world. There are those who can learn new tricks . . . no, ignore that . . . what I meant to say is there are those who can learn new things and there are those who either are not able to learn new things or choose not to. I'd like to think you are the kind of boys who can learn new things."

All the boys nodded "Yes" and some said it aloud.

"God can really use boys like you because there are a lot of things God wants to teach you. That is, in fact, one of the main reasons God sent his Son, Jesus into the world: So God could teach us how we are supposed to live.

"Living life the Jesus way does not come naturally or easily to most of us. Just like Nicky and Mitzi, we have to learn how to live this way. Then we have to practice it over and over again, until we are able to do it well all the time.

"Learning from Jesus how to love God and love our neighbor is what being a disciple of Jesus is all about. A lot of people listen to Jesus and know how he wants them to live, but they don't live it out very well because they do not care enough to practice it over and over again until they get it right. I want all of you to learn from Jesus, and then I want you to go to church and, along with everyone else who goes there, I want you to practice living like Jesus at church and at home, too. And school. And wherever else you might be. I want you to be good disciples. And I bet Jesus wants you to be good disciples, too.

"All right, let me introduce my final friend. Come on out and say, Hi!"

A small skinny dog with very large paws came walking out onto the platform. LaShaun had never seen a dog like this before. The dog stood up on his hind legs and walked clear across to Monica. He turned towards the audience and, still standing on his hind legs, he raised one of his paws and waved.

"This is my best friend, Bonker. Bonker is very clever and can do a lot of things. For example . . . Bonker, how do you get to work each morning?"

The dog got down on all four legs and walked over to the little tricycle. He sat on the seat, put his front paws on the handlebars and his back feet on the pedals and started peddling around the platform, peddling and steering at the same time.

"Good dog," Monica said as she tossed him a doggie treat. "Now show us what you do when you come to a river?"

Bonker got off the tricycle and walked over to the small tight rope. He climbed up a small set of stairs and put his front paw on the rope . . . then his other front paw and then, very quickly, he stepped out with all four legs and ran all the way across the rope without falling off.

"Wow," said Monica. "It's always a good idea to cross a river by using the bridge," and she tossed another treat through the air.

"But what do you do if there's no bridge? Go ahead, Bonker, show us what you do when there's no bridge."

Bonker dropped to the floor and, reaching one front leg out and then the other, he half-crawled and half-"swam" across the platform.

"Swimming is another good way to cross a river. But, now that we are almost done, can you show us what you do when you get to work?"

Bonker stood up on his rear legs again and began to twirl around like an ice skater doing her final spin . . . except a lot slower.

"As you can see, Bonker wants to be a ballet dancer when she grows up. Who knows? If she keeps practicing every day, she might dance the *Nutcracker Suite* some Christmas!"

The boys who knew what the *Nutcracker* was smiled and laughed. The other boys weren't sure what was so funny but they laughed anyway.

After Bonker had been sent back through the door Monica said, "If you want to be a disciple of Jesus you had better start practicing right now. You will need to practice being polite to each other. You will need to practice how to say 'I'm sorry' and 'I forgive you.' You will need to practice taking care of people who can't take care of themselves, like babies. You will need to practice sharing your money and time with other people who need it more than you do. You need to practice reading the Bible so you can learn what sort of things you need to be practicing!

"Someone once said, 'You can't teach an old dog new tricks.' This isn't true. I have found that any dog can learn to do something new if they decide they want to. The same is true for you. You are never too old or too young to start being a disciple of Jesus. So, learn the way of life that Jesus wants you to live and then practice, practice, practice.

"Oh, and one more thing: Did you notice the doggie treats I gave out as a reward for my friends when they did their best? Well, God hands out 'treats' for you, too, when you begin to live out the Jesus way of life. God gives you the biggest treat of all when you decide to be a disciple of Jesus. God gives you the forgiveness and salvation that Jesus won for you on the cross. But there are other treats God gives you along the way. There are the gifts of joy, peace, hope love, patience and love, kindness, goodness, faithfulness, gentleness, and self-control. They might not sound like treats to you but I can assure you that when God tosses one of them in the air in your direction you will find it to be the most wonderful thing you have ever tasted in your life!

"Nicky, Mitzi and Bonker all want to say 'Thank you' for being such a good audience. And I want to say, 'Thank you,' too. Have a great time at camp. And don't forget to practice!"

And with that she followed her dogs through the door and all the boys clapped and clapped.

When they were through clapping Fil stood up and said, "Now we are going to switch places with the girls. It's still raining so let's not take too much time to get over to the Dining Hall."

Everyone piled out of the Chapel in record time. Some of the boys ran but most of them, like LaShaun, just walked as fast as they could so they wouldn't get too wet. When they got to the Dining Hall the girls were just leaving so they had to wait outside for a little while until they could get through the doors.

LaShaun and Marcy saw each other at the same time and they both smiled and waved to each other.

Glen leaned over and said, "Who's that? Your girlfriend?" and then in a louder voice, "Does LaShaun have a girl friend?"

He thought he was going to embarrass him but LaShaun just looked at him and said, "Yeah, she's my girlfriend. What's the big deal about that?"

As they walked through the doors all Glen could think was, "Oh, wow, LaShaun has a girlfriend . . . that's kinda cool!"

They noticed the tables were now turned sideways and there were chairs only on the sides of the tables that faced the front of the hall. A big projector screen had been pulled down from the ceiling and LaShaun wondered why he had never noticed it before.

The camp director was standing there with a microphone and said, "Hello, boys. We are going to see a special short movie about a place called Haiti. Yesterday, Mr. Marshall told us about his ministry in Nigeria. Nigeria is in Africa, a long way from the United States. But Haiti is very close to our country. In fact, it is closer to Miami, Florida, than we are to Seattle, Washington.

"Haiti is a very poor country. It is, in fact, the poorest county in our whole half of the world from Canada to the tip of South America. Haiti is not only poor but several years ago they had a terrible earthquake that destroyed many buildings in the capital city. Millions of people lost their homes and have been living in tents or shacks ever since.

LaShaun wondered when the man was going to stop talking and show the video.

"The United States government came and helped out with a lot of things for several years. But then they got involved in helping out other places in the world and stopped helping Haiti. Most of the groups that stayed in Haiti and who are still there helping the people are Christian organizations that provide food, medicine, tents and blankets. They also help with rebuilding houses for people to live in and create businesses so people will have some place to work.

"Our movie shows what one of these Christian groups is doing there."

The boys tried to be polite but most of them were so bored that they all tried to go to the bathroom as often as possible. Some of them felt that standing outside in the rain would be more fun than watching the movie. They all sort-of watched as the movie showed lots of sad-looking children and lots and lots of rubble. Good people were doing good things for

God in Haiti but few of the boys were paying much attention to it. Even LaShaun kept thinking about what his next story was going to be and, when he wasn't thinking about that, he was thinking about Marcy or about wanting to stay at the camp with Fil for the rest of the summer. In a way LaShaun watched the movie but he didn't really see much of it.

After what seemed to be a thousand hours the movie came to an end. It had only been thirty-five minutes but that didn't matter. Everyone was just glad it was over. But it didn't take long before the boys figured out why the girls had seen the movie first . . . it was so the boys would be the ones to rearrange all the tables and chairs for lunch.

In just a few minutes the camp bell rang out and just as quickly the girls started streaming back into the Dining Hall. LaShaun was already in the lunch line but the camp director told all the boys to let the girls go first. Most of the boys quietly groaned and complained to each other about it, but LaShaun remembered what Monica had said about practicing what Jesus would do. He hoped he would get the gifts of patience and self-control right away!

Chapter Twelve
There Was a Dream
Thursday Afternoon

Soon it was the boys' turn to get their lunch and, in a few minutes, LaShaun and his cabin friends were back at their table eating macaroni and cheese with peas and red Jell-O. By the time they finished and started to clean up there were still a lot of peas left on their plates.

After lunch, everyone headed off for their afternoon electives. Because of the rain the "Sports" group did ping-pong under the tent and the "Camp Craft" group practiced lighting a campfire with wet wood. The Music group met as usual in the Chapel and the Writing group met in the back corner of the Dining Hall. Since they were going to get wet anyway

LaShaun's swimming class picked up right where they had left off the day before.

"Today," the teacher said, "I want you to float on your stomachs and kick with your legs."

LaShaun was surprised at how fast he moved through the water. Then, while they were still on their stomachs, the teacher had them practice reaching out and pulling back their arms like they had learned to do the day before. Some of the kids, like LaShaun, reached their arms way out and others just reached out a little bit under the water and moved their hands in a way the teacher called doing a "dog paddle." Either way, the kids were moving around in the pool bumping into each other and having a great time.

"Now," the teacher announced, "I want you to float, swim and kick all at the same time."

Water flew all over the place and several of the swimmers got water up their noses and down their throats. There was lots of coughing and gagging going on but LaShaun began to feel as though he had been doing it all his life. The teacher told him that he was taking to swimming like a fish takes to water. LaShaun wasn't exactly sure what that meant but he assumed it meant he was learning how to swim.

Marcy was doing well, too. One time she and LaShaun swam into each other, bumped heads and got all tangled up. LaShaun was ready to get all upset with whoever ran into him but when he saw it was Marcy he just laughed.

After that, the two of them found an empty corner of the pool and tried racing each other from one side to the other. They didn't go very fast but they were getting better at it each time they tried, and both of them were thinking about Monica's words: "practice, practice, practice!" It made them both smile to think they were like dogs learning a new trick!

Towards the end of class, the kids lined up along the edge of the pool while the teacher worked with them one at a time. She finished just as the camp bell rang to announce the beginning of free time.

"I'll see you tomorrow," she said. "You are all doing so well!"

While they were swimming, the rain stopped and the sun started to break through the clouds. Everything was still wet but the camp was bright and cheery again—except for the campfire circle. There, a huge pillar of wet, damp smoke was spewing out from the fire the "Camp Craft" group had tried to make.

Marcy and LaShaun decided to head straight down to the beach after their swimming class. Since most of the other kids had to change into their swimsuits, they were the first ones there.

"I wish I had taken the Kayak Water Safety class," LaShaun said. "Then we could paddle out into the lake. But it's too late in the week to do it now."

"That's okay," Marcy said. "Let's see if we can swim!"

The water in the lake was a lot colder than in the pool. The skin on their arms got lots of goose bumps and they shivered until they finally got brave enough to sit down in the water. After that the water didn't seem quite as cold. Marcy was the first to put her head under the water. She floated and swam with her arms and kicked with her feet, but only in the shallow areas where her feet could still reach the bottom. LaShaun followed her in and the two of them practiced swimming together along the edge of the beach.

After a while, they both stopped swimming and looked out in the lake where the diving platform was floating out in the deeper water.

"Well, Marcy, do you want to try swimming out to the raft?"

Marcy thought about it for a minute before saying, "No. I don't think I'm ready for that yet. Do you?"

"No, not really," LaShaun replied. "But I hope we can do it before we leave on Saturday."

"If we don't do it today then we will have to do it tomorrow," added Marcy. "I'm not sure I will be ready by then, either."

LaShaun added, "Well, like the Bible says, 'Where there's a will there's a way.'"

But Marcy said, "No, silly. That's not in the Bible."

She thought about what she had just said and then added, "But just because it isn't in the Bible doesn't mean it isn't true."

LaShaun was sure it was in the Bible somewhere so he made a mental note to look it up or ask Fil about it later.

As they were talking, some of the bigger kids ran into the water and swam straight out to the diving platform. It looked so easy for them and it didn't look like it was really very far away.

So LaShaun said, "I'm going to swim out there now. I know I can do it."

Marcy looked terrified. "No, LaShaun. Don't do it. You're crazy. You don't swim well enough. You'll drown, and I don't want you to drown!"

LaShaun didn't want to drown either but it seemed like Marcy cared even more about it than he did. It sounded as though losing him would be a terrible thing for her. For the first time all week it dawned on him that he was really important to Marcy and that they had become friends in a way he would not have thought possible just a few days ago.

Back then he had wondered if there would ever be a girl who would love him and now here was Marcy.

Maybe she loved him and maybe she didn't. But that didn't really matter. What mattered was that Marcy cared what happened to him.

"Okay," is what he said, "Let's wait until tomorrow and see if we can do it together."

Marcy smiled and took his hand in hers and gave it a little squeeze. LaShaun felt as though something suddenly changed inside of him. It was as though he didn't feel like a child any more. He didn't think he felt like an adult might feel but sort of something in between. It was a very confusing feeling.

He had thought that maybe when he became a teenager he might feel things like this, but he was still only twelve years old . . . well almost thirteen.

He gave Marcy's hand a squeeze and was a little disappointed when she pulled her hand back and said, "I'm getting cold. Let's get some hot chocolate!"

The "Snack Shack" was only a few steps away so they wrapped themselves up in their towels and walked over together.

"This is on me," LaShaun said.

He had heard his father say this lots of times but it was the first time he had ever said it. It came out sounding sort of goofy but Marcy said,

"That's really nice of you, LaShaun. Thank you."

He thought she might have taken a small step closer to him when she said it and that stirred up another new feeling, a feeling he liked a lot.

When they first arrived at camp all the kids put money aside for snacks and souvenirs so LaShaun didn't have to pay anything for the hot chocolate. The counselor in the booth just charged it to his account. This was still another thing that made him feel more grown up than he had ever felt before in his life. Maybe, he thought, he would have to start shaving soon! But he felt his face and decided that maybe he wasn't quite ready for that . . . yet!

They took their hot chocolate and sat next to each other on a nearby log. LaShaun had never sat this close to a girl before, especially on a beach wearing swimsuits and without being a part of a big group of kids hanging around with each other. For the second time that week he wondered if this was like a date and the idea of kissing Marcy rolled around in his brain like a bird that flies in through an open window and can't find its way out again.

So they sat and sipped their hot chocolate and felt warm and talked about places they had been and things they dreamed of doing and each of them imagined that one day they might be doing those things together but they didn't say any of that out loud.

For a while they just sat there without talking.

LaShaun started to get up to toss his empty cup into a trash bin but Marcy held on to his arm and said, "LaShaun, you are one of the nicest people I have ever known. And the best friend I have ever had at camp . . . any camp."

She sat there as if there was more that she wanted to say but the words didn't show up.

Finally, she said, "Hey, you told me that your cabin tells stories every night? Do you tell stories, too?"

LaShaun thought it was funny that everything that happened all week seemed to have something to do with stories, but he did his best to answer her question.

"Yes, I guess I do tell stories. I told one couple of nights ago. But the first one was on Monday during our afternoon cabin time. I'd never told a story out loud before and it turned out really well. Fil said that maybe it was a God thing. I don't know about that. How about you, do you like stories?"

Instead of answering the question, Marcy asked one of her own: "Will you tell me a story? Right now? Will you tell me one?"

And, right there, while sitting on a log with Marcy, with kids running and screaming all around them, LaShaun was surprised to hear himself starting to tell a story he had never heard before. It felt to him as

137

though Marcy had pushed a button on a vending machine and, instead of a bag of chips, a story just fell out. This is what he heard.

"There was a dream and there was a young girl who dreamed it. In the dream there was a bird and the bird was beautiful. It was blue. Its head was red and there were long, delicate feathers of green and gold above its eyes and along its back.

"In the dream the bird flew high in the sky and the girl flew along with it. The houses and trees became small, the rivers looked like streams and the lakes became the size of ponds. There was silence everywhere, except for the sound of the air itself which whispered stories and dreams to them as it passed by; stories of the wind and the earth, the sea and the sky.

"As the bird and the girl soared together, it was as though they were no longer in the world at all. Nor did they feel they were in the sky; for they had drifted into a new world where there was no earth or sky but simply the place where they were. In the dream the bird was joined by other birds, each completely different but equally beautiful.

"As the girl watched, their faces become the faces of her family and friends. And there were faces of people she had never seen before; faces of people from all over the world. Yet each of them and all of them together seemed to be at peace with each other and she felt as though she loved them all. She had never before felt so loved, so completely happy or so free.

"As she watched, the faces became once again the faces of birds and, one by one, they either flew away or simply disappeared, she couldn't really tell because that is the way it is with dreams. Then she was alone with the one bird whose face had never changed and she wondered who the bird might be. But as she wondered, and as she dreamed, the air became cold and she began to tremble. The new-born world of her dream began to dissolve, and it dissolved until all that remained was the wind and the earth, the sea and the sky.

"She followed the bird back to the place where her dream had begun. The bird bowed its head to her and then, without a word or a sound, disappeared. She awoke from her dream. And when she awoke, she found her world was the same but no longer the same. In the same way, she found she was also the same but no longer the same. Although she had awakened from her dream, she found that the dream remained, and had become a part of her forever."

LaShaun's mouth stayed open and he waited for more words to come out but they didn't. The story had come to an end and he found himself lost in wonder, lost in the story and lost in the dream that had become one with his own.

When he looked at Marcy she was crying softly and looking at him as though she was seeing him for the first time. Without saying a word, she leaned over and kissed him on the cheek. She smiled and stood; her hair radiant in the light of the midday sun. The camp bell rang and they awoke to find that they were no longer the same; and that the world had changed along with them.

It took a moment or two before they realized it was time to go back to their cabins. Neither of them wanted to go but they knew they had to. So Marcy headed back to her cabin and LaShaun hurried back to his.

He arrived just as Fil was about to lead the Elijah boys on an outing to find a picnic table or two. Fil had two plastic table cloths and several beach towels. He gave two of the boys the towels and a canvas bag to carry. When they found two picnic tables under some trees where it wasn't too muddy, Fil put on the tablecloths and had the boys dry the benches with the towels. The benches were still damp when they sat down but no one complained. Most of the boys had started to be bored by the camp until the hail and rain made it seem like more of an adventure again.

140

Everyone wondered what Fil had in the bag. He took out eight pairs of scissors, a bunch of different colored construction paper, a small bundle of toothpicks, four bottles of Elmer's Glue and then divided them up between the two tables.

"What I want you to do this afternoon is to design your personal 'Coat of Arms.' You know, like in the old days when kings and knights had special symbols and designs on their shields and stuff like that. It is called 'heraldry' and families that do genealogy are always excited when they discover their family crest for the first time. Here are a few examples of what Coats of Arms look like.

"It's usually some sort of shield with different symbols on it that tell something about the person who owns it. If you love horses you might want to put a horse on it, you get the idea. If there are three of you in your family you could put three stars on it. Most Coats of Arms have one or more lines running through it to divide it in half or into three or four parts. This way there can be more symbols and designs."

Fil held up some more drawings.

"Here are some examples of what that looks like. Okay, here are some pencils for you to draw with. And don't make your shield too small or else it will be hard to put any symbols on it."

141

Then in a very fast voice he said, "One-two-three-go!"

And all the boys started grabbing paper and started drawing and cutting out the particular shapes and symbols they had chosen.

Garret raised his hand and asked, "Fil? What is the glue for?"

Marty interrupted him by saying, "It's to glue your symbols onto your shield . . . duh!"

LaShaun decided he would divide his shield down the middle into two parts. On the left side he carefully put three stars; two at the top for him and his Dad and one at the bottom for his Mom. On the other side he wanted to put something that would represent a story. He wanted it to be the kind of story that someone tells but he couldn't figure out how to cut out a mouth or to show a face with words coming out of it. So, he finally gave up and cut out something that looked like an open book. He had to do some drawing on it with his pencil to make it look right but when he had finished, he thought looked just the way he wanted.

He wanted to put Marcy on there, too, but he couldn't figure out where. He thought he could add her as a fourth star but that was family and Marcy wasn't family. The thought of her being family crossed his mind but he let the thought go and, in the end, decided to cut out one more star and glue it onto the middle of the book.

After a while Fil said, "How many of you have finished your Coat of Arms?"

Five hands went up so he said, "Now you're ready for the final part of this project. Put a large drop of glue on the front of your shield and smear it all around with a toothpick. It will look all white and gluey but don't worry. When it dries it will be clear. It will make the shield stiffer and keep water from messing it up. We'll only do the front today. Tomorrow it will be dry enough for us to do the same thing to the back."

Putting the glue on didn't take very long so LaShaun walked around and looked at the pine needles and the oak leaves nearby and wondered how God managed to make things like trees that looked so much alike but were so different from each other.

When everyone was done with their craft, Fil explained that this had been one of the crafts they didn't do on Tuesday because everyone was so tired.

"But I think that is enough for today. Just lay your shield on the tray face up so it dries without sticking to anything."

He put all the stuff back in the bag and gave the bag and the tray to Robert and Marty to take back to the cabin. As the boys were leaving, he called for

LaShaun to come over and then asked him to sit down with him at one of the tables.

"LaShaun," he began. "There's something I want to tell you. I probably shouldn't but I think that you will . . . uh . . . I think that it will be all right . . . to tell you . . . something about me."

LaShaun sat there not knowing if he should say anything or not.

"What I want to say is . . . well, do you remember the story you told on Monday about the stone and the boy?"

LaShaun nodded head, thinking how in the world could he forget something like that.

"You might have noticed that afterward I had trouble talking and that I ended the story time. Well, there was a reason for that. You see the story you told about the boy was all about me. It was my story you told. You didn't know it but it was.

"Like the boy in your story my Dad died when I was twelve years old. My Mom and I had to move away and live with my aunt and uncle just like in your story. My prayers weren't answered either. But my Mom kept taking me to church anyway and, like Ralph said the other night, going to summer Bible camps helped me get back in touch with God and with Jesus. It was hard for me to listen to your story . . . ."

LaShaun interrupted him to say, "I'm sorry; I'm really sorry that I told the story. I didn't mean to hurt you . . . I didn't know . . . ."

But Fil cut him off and said, "No. Don't feel sorry about it. Your story was a story from God to me. It hurt to hear it but it also reminded me about how God brought so many good things into my life because of it . . . I mean . . . because of my father . . . you know . . . dying and everything."

"And," he added, "that's the other thing I want to tell you. Remember the long talk we had on Tuesday?"

LaShaun wondered how he could ever forget that, either.

"Well, when I asked you what good God could bring out of what happened with your Mother and Father you said that maybe, because of it, you could help other kids who were going through the same thing."

LaShaun nodded as a way to let Fil know he was listening and wanted him to keep talking.

"Well, that broke me up, too, because that is what I decided to do after my Dad died. That's one of the reasons I like being a counselor at the camp each summer. I get to meet kids like you and talk about things like this.

"But there is something different about you, LaShaun. Instead of me helping you, it seems as though maybe we have been helping each other. Your stories have really helped me think about things and . . . uh . . . I guess I just wanted to say, 'Thank you,' and to encourage you to keep telling stories. I think God is already using you to help other people, and . . . and . . .I guess that's all I wanted to say."

LaShaun didn't know what to say. Fil had been a real friend to him all week. In fact, LaShaun had decided that when he grew up, he wanted to be just like Fil. Now here was Fil telling him, in a strange sort of way, that he was already like him.

Fil may have said it, but LaShaun didn't feel like it. He was still only a kid who didn't even know what was going on with himself. How could he be helping anyone else? He was the one who needed help!

So LaShaun just sat there feeling all twisted up until Fil said, "Anything you want to say, LaShaun?"

But LaShaun just shook his head, "No," and the two of them walked down to dinner together.

Chapter Thirteen
Once There Was a River
Thursday Evening

Dinner was lasagna. LaShaun felt hungrier than he had all week. He ate the dinner so quickly that he was back in line hoping for seconds before all the rest of the kids had gone through the first time. There had been so much that had happened that day and the days before, that he couldn't get all the feelings and thoughts straight. He decided he wanted to meet with Fil and talk things over with him again.

When he saw Marcy eating with her friends, he brought his second helping of lasagna over to her table and sat across from her.

"Hi," he said.

This was the first time he had seen Marcy since she kissed him on the cheek earlier in the afternoon so he was all confused about that, too. But as usual, Marcy said all the right things to make him feel comfortable again.

"Hi, back at ya," she said with a smile and a wink that made LaShaun worry that everyone in the Dining Hall had seen it.

But the wink made him smile back and, although he spent most of the next ten minutes staring at his lasagna, he felt as though he would rather be sitting here with Marcy than be anywhere else in the world.

Corinne asked LaShaun what his group did in the afternoon and he said they made family "coats of arms."

Corinne said that the girls made small boxes to put things in when they got home.

"They gave us some scripture verses to choose from, printed on special paper. I chose the verse from last night's campfire talk; the one about Jesus and living life to the full."

Millie added, "Then we glued the paper on top of the box and covered the whole thing with Elmer's Glue."

Marcy joined in the conversation by explaining how Tracy had said the glue would be clear once it dried. She wasn't sure because she had never thought about using glue for something like that before.

LaShaun asked her what verse she had chosen and she said, "The one from when Jesus was born that goes, 'Glory to God in the highest, and on earth, peace."

She said it reminded her of the story LaShaun had told her that afternoon.

LaShaun still wasn't exactly sure what his story meant but he was glad it meant something to Marcy.

He also wasn't sure what to say next so he said, "That was good lasagna, wasn't it?"

"Yes it was," said Marcy.

"The best I ever had," LaShaun added.

The conversation might have gone on like this all night, but the camp bell rang and they had to get up and get ready for the campfire program.

LaShaun and Marcy walked to the campfire together as if it was the most normal thing in the world and, at that moment in time, it was. As they sat waiting, LaShaun wanted to share with Marcy what Fil had said to him about LaShaun's story matching up with his life, but he didn't know if it was right to share something that private and personal. If Marcy asked about it, he wondered how he would do the "Yes" or "No" thing that Jesus had taught his disciples.

Do I have to tell the truth about everything all the time? he wondered. Or were there exceptions, like keeping a friend's secret to yourself?

He didn't come up with an answer because Worthy stood up and said that Michelle, the counselor of the Lydia cabin, had some things to say.

Everyone wondered what it was until Michelle stood up and asked, "How well do you know your Bible?"

The kids sat as if their mouths had suddenly been taped shut.

"Well then, let's see what you know: Who was the greatest banker in the Bible?"

One of the kids caught on immediately and raised his hand saying, "I know! I know!"

Michelle asked him for the answer and he said, "Pharaoh's daughter; because she pulled a small prophet from a rush on the banks!"

Michelle and a few of the other kids started laughing but most of the others weren't sure what was so funny.

"That's a good answer," Michelle said, "But you could also say that Noah was even better,"

"Why?" the kids shouted.

"Because Noah floated a-loan while the rest of the world was liquidated!"

This time no one laughed because no one got the joke except the other counselors.

"All right," she went on, "Let's try this one: Who was the first pharmacist in the Bible?"

No one raised their hands so she said, "It was Moses, because he brought the tablets down from the mountain!"

By now most of the kids knew she was telling jokes and since none of them wanted to look as though they were stupid everyone started laughing as though they knew what she was talking about.

"One more," she said. "When is the first car mentioned in the Bible?"

"Tell us!" the kids shouted.

"On Pentecost, when the Bible says that the disciples were all in "one accord!"

There was a brief moment of silence and then everybody started laughing again.

"Thank you, Michelle!" said Worthy. "Now let's praise the Lord!"

After a few songs and a prayer, Fil walked up to the front.

"My name is Fil and I'm the counselor with the Elijah cabin. I've been having a fun time but I really want to tell you that I have seen God in a lot of places this week—and in a lot of people, too.

"In my cabin we like to tell stories or listen to them. I've told most of the stories but my kids have told some, too."

"It all reminds me of Jesus, who liked to tell stories. He told stories everywhere he went. The Bible

151

calls most of these stories "parables" which is a fancy name for the type of story that Jesus liked to tell most. Most parables tell a story and then just sort of end without telling you what they mean, or why Jesus told them in the first place. When a parable came out of Jesus' mouth, it just sort of hung in the air like fruit hanging on a tree, waiting for someone to pick it and try to eat it.

"When I read these parables of Jesus, sometimes I understand what they mean and sometimes I don't. Later, when I read them for the second or third time, some of the harder ones start to make sense. Some of the stories in our cabin were like that. When I heard them, I wasn't sure what they meant or whether they meant anything at all. But after a while they started to mean something to me. I mean they started to mean a *lot* to me.

LaShaun shifted nervously on the bench, worried that Fil was going say his name.

"I think," Fil continued, "that what I'm trying to say is that our whole Christian faith is like that sometimes. Some things we understand and other things just sort of hang there in front of us but we don't know exactly what they are, or whether they are something we should be picking and eating or not. Later, though, when we go back and look at them again—like maybe when we are a little older and know more things about life and death and things like that—we start to understand them better.

"Sometimes, we find that the things we didn't understand the first time around turn out to be some of the most important things in our lives. God is patient and wise enough to let us know what they mean when we really need to know. At least that is how it has been in my life.

Some of the kids started looking at each other, wondering if anyone knew what Fil was talking about.

"I have learned things this week that I have never understood before. I have learned them from some of our speakers and from some of the questions you have asked and even from some of the stupid things I have said or done that were all messed up.

"But the best part has been the stories. I hope that, when you go home, you will tell your families lots of stories about this week at camp. I hope you will tell these stories over and over again until they start to make sense to you. I say this because I think God gave the stories to you as a gift; a gift you should treasure."

Without saying anything else, Fil just sort of stepped back and walked away.

Worthy said, "Well that will give us a lot to think about, won't it?"

She sounded as though she didn't quite understand what Fil had been talking about, either, but as far as Fil

153

was concerned, that didn't matter. Sooner or later, if it really did matter, God would open her heart and let her know what his words might mean for her.

LaShaun was embarrassed by what he heard, because he knew that a lot of what Fil talked about had to do with himself. But he also knew that Fil was telling everybody not to worry about the things that didn't seem to make sense. If it was important for them to know, God would help them know what they needed to know, when they needed to know it.

There was so much about the week that LaShaun didn't understand. Fil's little talk helped him to feel it might be okay if he didn't understand all of it right away. With God's help, LaShaun hoped he would be able to put the pieces together later.

The campfire time was over and all the kids went back to their cabins. Before he left LaShaun looked over and saw Marcy studying him again as though he was a mystery to be solved.

"It's all right," she said. "I think I understand more than you think I do."

Along with everything else, LaShaun didn't understand what Marcy had just said, either. But he reached out his hand to hers and gave her hand a little squeeze like she had given him earlier that day. He wasn't even exactly sure why he did it or what he meant by it but it just seemed to be the right thing to do.

As it turned out, Marcy felt the same way and she smiled all the way back to her cabin.

Back at the Elijah cabin, LaShaun walked in and was surprised to see Robert and Marty talking to Fil about what he had just said at the campfire.

"That made a lot of sense," he heard Marty say. "There is so much in the Bible, and in all the other stuff that people keep telling me about being a Christian, that I don't get. Even a lot of the things that Jesus said—I don't understand it. But each year that I come to camp I learn a little bit more. And this week, a lot of it started to make sense for the first time."

Robert said pretty much the same thing: "My Dad's a pastor and I have had to go to church every Sunday and go to Bible camp every summer and most of it hasn't made a whole lot of sense to me, either. But I have been thinking about that story you told about the kite thing and about what LaShaun was saying about the man knocking on the doors and I'm beginning to understand some things about Jesus that I never understood before. I know the week isn't over yet but both of us, Marty and me, just wanted to let you know that we're glad we came to camp this summer and we're both glad that you're our counselor."

They both looked a little embarrassed to be talking to Fil like that but Fil listened to them until they were finished and then said, "Can I pray with you about this?"

Marty and Robert looked at each other as though they weren't sure it was a good idea to do it in front of all the other kids but Fil didn't give them a chance to say anything.

He just put his hands on their shoulders and prayed, "Dear Jesus, Thank you for touching Marty and Robert with your love this week. Make them good and strong disciples so they will serve you well for the rest of their lives. In Jesus' name I pray. Amen."

Robert and Marty looked at each other again and then took a step back before turning around and heading over to their bunks.

All the other kids just stood around thinking about what Marty, Robert and Fil had said. They also wondered about the stories they had heard that week. For some of them, the fun stories they had heard at the beginning of the week didn't seem to be as important as they had a few days ago. They wanted to hear more stories like the ones LaShaun had told and like the one that Fil had told about the boy and the kite.

Every boy in the cabin seemed to have something to write in their journal that night. LaShaun filled in over two pages with things that had happened that day. Fil watched them write and wondered what they were writing about. He would have been surprised and amazed if he had known.

After everyone had been to the bathroom they changed and climbed into bed. For many of them this had become the best part of the day.

Even before Fil had turned off the lights Glen said, "Tell us a story. Someone tell us a story."

Phil added, "Anyone at all, tell us a story!"

And Colin said, "I'll tell you a story."

The whole room became quiet because Colin hadn't said much about anything all week.

He had hung out with Mo, Phil and LaShaun at the Dining Hall but that was about all any of the other boys knew about him except that he had been to Europe. Even LaShaun didn't know much about him even though they ate together and their beds were next to each other.

"Well," Fil said, "if you have a story you'd like to tell, we'd like to hear it. Right you guys?"

Some weren't so sure they wanted to hear Colin's story and others thought that if Colin told a long story than there wouldn't be enough time left to hear one from Fil or LaShaun.

But all of them said, "Sure, Colin. What's your story? We want to hear it."

"Go ahead, Colin,"

Fil asked, "Do you want the lights on or off?"

Colin said he would like them to be off, so Fil did the usual countdown from ten and when he came to zero, the lights went out. After a moment or two Colin started to tell his story.

"Once there was a river. It was a big river. No, I mean, it was a small river that was just the size you could throw a rock across if you threw it as hard as you could. There were rocks in the river and although there were deep places where the water moved fast, it was possible, if you were very careful, to walk across the river on the rocks without getting your feet wet.

"There was a boy who loved to play around the river. He was very good with the rocks and could run back and forth across the river as fast as the wind could blow. But one day something went wrong. One rock came loose and wiggled as he put his foot on it. His ankle twisted, his arms flew out and all of him fell into the water with a gigantic splash. He went completely under the water but, when he pulled himself out, he seemed to be only very wet and nothing about him appeared to be any different than before.

"But something had changed. The boy's hair began to grow, and it grew quickly—beautiful hair that would not stop growing. The boy's mother would cut

158

it in the morning and by bedtime she would need to cut it again. The hair fell into his eyes and caught in the door and, when he went to bed, he was afraid that it would strangle him while he was asleep.

"Even cutting all of it off didn't keep it from growing back. The boy's parents tried chemicals and they even tried pulling it out by the roots but this only seemed to make it grow faster than before. Growing the hair took so much energy out of the boy that he became very weak and felt tired all of the time.

"One day, when everyone had given up all hope, the boy's hair stopped growing. It still grew, of course, but not quite as fast as before. This made the boy feel much better and soon he began walking and then running and playing outdoors again.

"Then, for some reason that no one could understand, the hair started growing again. And the boy began to feel tired. One day when he could hardly stand up, he slowly and painfully made his way down to the river. But the hair had grown around his legs and as he came to the river he tripped and fell into the water and was swept away, never to be seen again."

There was silence, and the boys kept waiting for more but Colin had stopped and had nothing more to say.

"Is that it?" someone said.

"What sort of a story is that?" said another.

"What a dumb story" said a third.

Fil turned the light back on and walked over to Colin's bunk. Colin was sitting up and didn't look very good at all.

Fil got down on his knees and took Colin's hand in his own.

"That was a hard story for you to tell, wasn't it?"

Colin nodded his head and Fil could see tears forming in his eyes.

"The story was about you, wasn't it?"

Colin nodded his head a second time.

"Colin, your hair looks just fine. Is there something else that is growing?"

As Colin nodded his head for the third time he began to sob. The tears came and wouldn't stop. The boys didn't know what to think, what to say or what to do.

Mo, who had been the one to say he thought the story was "dumb," climbed down from his bunk, hurried over to Colin and said, "Hey, Colin. I'm sorry I said your story was dumb. I didn't mean to say that. I guess I just didn't understand what it . . . the story . . . I mean it was your story and I should have liked it. I'm sorry I said it was dumb."

Colin stopped sobbing long enough to say, "It's okay, Mo. It's not your fault. It is a dumb story but there's nothing that I can do about it."

160

Fil asked all the boys to come over and stand around Colin's bunk so they could say a prayer together. Colin wasn't sitting up any more. He had buried his head in his pillow.

Fil put his hand on his back and began to pray: "Lord, I don't . . . we don't know why Colin is so upset but it must be something really big to make him this unhappy. Lord Jesus, touch him just like I am touching him now. Dry his tears and give him the comfort and love that only you can give. Help us to be here for Colin even though we don't yet understand what is going on. Fill him with love and peace. I ask this in Jesus' name. Amen."

When the prayer was over, Colin gave a few more sobs, then a few sniffles and then, very slowly, he lifted his head up from the pillow and sat up again.

"Thanks for the prayer. I'm glad you let me tell my story. I knew you would listen even though I didn't know if you would understand it or not. But now that I've done it, I feel a little better. You've been my family and friends this week . . ."

Colin began crying again but not as much as before.

Fil asked, "Do you want to tell us about the story? We aren't sure what it means. But we'd like to know . . . if you're willing to tell us."

161

Colin looked straight into Fil's eyes and, in a voice that only Fil and a few of the boys closest to the bed could hear, said, "I have cancer and I'm going to die."

Several boys said, "What did he say? I couldn't hear it."

The ones who had heard began whispering what Colin had said until everyone in the room had heard about it. Mo started to cry and Glen felt sick and left for the bathroom in a hurry.

Everyone else just sat and stared at each other, stared at the floor, or just kept their eyes closed while Fil talked quietly with Colin.

Colin explained that two years ago, he had gotten weaker and weaker and when the doctors looked him over, they found a large tumor growing in his intestines. They did a test and found it was cancer. They had surgery and cut it out and then did radiation and chemotherapy treatments. Instead of his hair growing like in the story, it all fell out and for six months he was completely bald. For a while he felt much better and his hair grew back. He felt good enough to go to Europe and to ask his parents if he could go to Bible camp. They weren't sure it was a good idea but they sent in his registration anyway.

The week before camp the doctors told them the tumor was back. It was growing very fast and the cancer was now in his ribs and his liver. They said there was nothing more they could do except maybe slow it down a little and help with the pain when it started to hurt. His parents wanted him to stay home but he said he really wanted to go to camp. So, they talked to the camp director and the camp nurse and they decided to give it a try and see how it worked out. They signed him up for Creative Writing because he liked to write and because he wouldn't have to do anything physical that took up too much energy.

Colin said he had been having a great time at camp and still felt good. But as it got closer to the end of the week, he was beginning to realize that it was all going to end and then—well—then he would go home and he would never go to Bible camp again.

He had written his story as part of the Creative Writing class but he hadn't let anyone see it until now. He added that he felt lucky he had gotten into what he thought was the best cabin at the camp.

Fil asked if he wanted to talk to the camp director or make a phone call to his parents but he said, "No." He didn't want it to be a secret any more so the other guys didn't have to keep it one if they didn't want to.

Fil told everyone they could do whatever they wanted but that he felt it would be better for Colin if they kept it to themselves until Saturday morning when everyone went home.

Marty said he wasn't going to tell anyone and LaShaun said he wasn't going to say anything either, and, one by one, all the boys said the same.

Then Robert cut in and said, "We don't have to swear on a stack of Bibles, either. We can just let our 'Yes' be 'Yes' and our 'No' be 'No.' Right guys?"

They all said "Yes."

Colin whispered "Thank you," and then he curled up and fell asleep.

Garret spoke up and said, "What's going to happen to Colin?"

All the boys looked at Fil who took a while to decide what to say.

"I don't know what is going to happen to Colin," is what he finally said. "But I know God will be with him and with his family, too. No matter how hard or how sad it gets, I know God will be with them for as long as it takes.

"It's not easy to think about it, but every one of us will die someday. So, it is good to know that Jesus, when he died, didn't stay dead. It's as though Jesus said, 'Don't worry too much about it. There is more to come!'

"Actually, Jesus put it this way, 'Don't get all upset about what will happen to me after I die. First, I'll come back to see you one more time and then I will go on ahead and get a room all fixed up for you so when the time comes, we can be in heaven together.'"

After a short pause, Fil added, "Well, that might not be exactly how he said it but . . . well . . . I guess it's close enough.

"What will happen to Colin will happen to all of us, sooner or later. But because of Jesus we know, that after all the sad and hard times are over, the story will have a happy ending.

"So, let's just let Colin enjoy himself for the rest of the week. Don't get all gushy over him. Just try to act the same way you've been acting and let God and Colin work the rest out between themselves? Are you going to be okay tonight?"

No one said anything so Fil said. "Well, if any of you change your mind just come over and wake me up. I won't mind and then we can talk or just be with each other for a while. Are there any questions or anything else you want to say?"

Once again, he waited but no one said anything.

"I think that Colin's story has been enough for tonight. Now go to sleep. But if you want to stay up and pray or read or something, you can use your flashlight and it will be alright.

"Good night . . . There's still more to do tomorrow so get some sleep."

And the lights went out.

A few flashlights lit up but after a short while, they went out too.

There was silence until the morning.

Chapter Fourteen
More Valuable than Gold
Friday Morning

When LaShaun woke up the sun was rising over the Sierras. He could tell it was going to be a hot day. He noticed that Colin and some of the other boys were already up and getting dressed.

"'Morning, Colin," he said.

Colin said, "Hey, LaShaun."

It was only then that LaShaun remembered what Colin had told them when they had gone to bed the night before. He felt really awkward and not sure what to say or what not to say. Since Colin seemed perfectly normal LaShaun figured he should just be normal, too.

What was it Fil had said? "Don't get all gushy over him!"

Well, thought LaShaun, *that won't be very hard to do!*

He couldn't even imagine what it would be like to "get all gushy" over someone; especially Colin!

Fil was up and dressed, too.

"Time for devotions," he said. "Stop where you are and sit down for a minute."

When all the boys were sitting or lying on their bunks Fil handed Phil his Bible and asked him to read from Isaiah 40:29-31.

> He gives strength to the weary
>   and increases the power of the weak.
> Even youths grow tired and weary,
>   and young men stumble and fall;
> but those who hope in the LORD
>   will renew their strength.
> They will soar on wings like eagles;
>   they will run and not grow weary,
>   they will walk and not be faint.

"Earlier this week," Fil said, "we heard LaShaun tell a story where a boy was able to fly. I don't know about you but I could imagine myself doing that and it was wonderful!

"What Phil just read, I don't think Isaiah is telling us that God can make us fly like birds; but I do think that Isaiah is telling us that God can take the weak things in us and make them strong.

"Jesus showed what this means when he healed the sick, made the blind to see and the lame to walk. It was just like Isaiah had promised: those who hoped in the Lord Jesus found that their strength was renewed. And I think that is still true for us today.

"Take your journal and write something about yourself that feels weaker than you would like it to be. And now write down what you would like God to do about it so you can grow stronger.

"Maybe you feel weak in faith or in patience or in forgiving someone. Maybe you feel too shy or too bossy. Whatever it is, it's should be something that you feel you aren't strong enough to change without God's help. So, in your journal ask Jesus to come alongside you and help you to sprout wings!"

After a few minutes Fil said, "Okay, boys. Put down those pencils. Let's spread out our wings and fly down to breakfast!

"What a great way to start off the day, by deciding that we want God to make us as spiritually and physically strong and healthy as possible."

As if it had been planned out in advance the camp bell rang and with Fil leading the way, the Elijah boys, including the older ones, ran all the way to the Dining Hall with their arms flapping.

LaShaun was glad Fil had read the Isaiah verses that morning because he was starting to feel "tired and weary" about this being the last full day of camp. His talks with Fil, the stuff about Colin, the stuff with Marcy, the swimming and the stories all had too many

169

loose ends dangling. He couldn't figure out how he was going to tie them all up in one day.

Breakfast was French toast with little smoked sausages and applesauce. For some reason, he didn't use syrup but just put some butter on the toast and ate it with his hands. He tried dipping it into the apple sauce but gave that up when it dripped all over his t-shirt.

Marty, Robert and Glen came over and sat with LaShaun, Phil, Mol and Colin. It made LaShaun feel good to see the older, bigger boys want to eat at his table. He wondered why? He wondered if it was because of Colin?

Marty popped a sausage into his mouth and then, while he was still chewing, said, "Robert and Glen and I are going to go forward at the campfire tonight when they ask for . . . well . . . to give your life to Jesus. What are you guys going to do?"

LaShaun felt as though someone had just tossed him another rock to juggle along with the others.

"I don't know," he said, "I haven't thought about it."

Colin said he was going to go and it crossed everyone's mind that this might be Colin's last chance to do it.

Phil said he had come forward every year he had been in camp and didn't see any reason not to do it again this year. For him it was sort of like renewing his subscription to *National Geographic*. He just wanted to say "Yes" to Jesus at least once a year when he had the chance. He said that at his church the pastor called people up to the altar every week and sometimes he went up and sometimes he didn't. He had done it so many times that it was no big deal.

"Except that it *is* a big deal, if you know what I mean."

LaShaun wasn't exactly sure he knew what Phil meant but he knew he could really use some help juggling all these rocks.

LaShaun was having a hard time thinking it out straight. He wondered if he might be able to say it better if he put it into a story.

As he thought about it, he looked up from his plate and there was Marcy standing there with Millie and Corinne.

"Tracy reminded us that this morning is when we get to do gold panning," Marcy said. "None of us have ever done that before. Have you?"

Robert, Marty and Phil all said they had but LaShaun and Colin said, "No," they had never done that before.

Robert said it was fun and that everybody got at least a small fleck of gold to take home.

LaShaun had visions of "Bent-Pan Billy" and the ping-pong sized nugget he had used to pay for his whisky. Maybe he would find a nugget like that!

"It's all just a set-up," said Marty. "They take some gold dust and sprinkle it into some dirt and then you get to swish it around in a pan until you find the gold. It's not like real gold panning in a stream but you do have to move the pan the right way to get the gold out of it. It'll be fun. Last year we did it over by the Director's Cabin, next to the parking lot."

The gold panning had been on the camp brochure and on the camp schedule that was handed out when the kids arrived, as well as being posted all over the camp where anyone could read it if they wanted to. Apparently LaShaun hadn't read any of it, because he had no idea, they were going to do gold panning until Marcy mentioned it. After hearing about it, it seemed like it would be a lot of fun.

After everyone walked over to the camp parking area, they were separated into cabin groups. There were four troughs filled with water and sand. They were only long enough for four kids to stand on each side so the four girl's cabins went first while the boys went off to the side to hear all about the gold rush.

LaShaun remembered when he had been in fourth grade. In California, that is when kids learn all about state history, including the Gold Rush. So LaShaun already knew about John Marshall discovering gold at Sutter's Mill in 1948, all the different ways people got to California and the different ways they looked for the gold.

As Mr. Buchannan talked, the only thing LaShaun could think about was Bent-Pan Billy and Lucky Lars. He had learned more about the Gold Rush from Fil's story than he had from his fourth-grade teacher and Mr. Buchannan combined!

The best part about Mr. Buchannan's presentation was when he pulled out a small clear plastic bottle with three real gold nuggets in it. They weren't the size of ping-pong balls but they were larger than a pencil eraser and they shone like . . . well . . . like gold in the morning sun!

Every so often, LaShaun could hear one of the girls give off a little shriek or a "Eureka" off in the distance.

He already knew that "Eureka" is the California State Motto, and that it is a Latin word meaning, "I have found it." He figured it was all about finding the gold. But maybe, for some people, just finding California had been a Eureka!

Soon it was the boys turn to learn how to pan and to try their luck at finding some gold.

"Keep in mind," they were told, "that because gold is heavy and sinks, and because the girls have stirred everything up, the gold has probably gone towards the bottom of the trough where it might be hard to get into your pans. So be sure to dig as deep into the sand as you can!"

Colin, who was standing across from LaShaun, was the first boy to find a fleck of gold. It was smaller than the head of a pin but it made him jump up and down as though he had found a fortune. One of the men helped him get it out of the pan and put it in a small plastic bottle to take home.

In a few minutes LaShaun found a tiny fleck of gold in his pan and, a few minutes later, all the boys had found one to put in their bottles.

The boys joined the girls just as Mr. Buchannan finished talking to them about the Gold Rush.

When everyone was seated, he asked, "We put one larger nugget in one of the troughs. Did one of you find it?"

One of the Lydia girls said she had found it and the man told her that it was probably worth around $150.

"There were over fifty of you panning for gold and only one of you found a nugget that was worth anything. That is how it was during the Gold Rush, too. Only a few found enough gold to pay their bills or to have enough food to eat. And even fewer actually made money out of it. After three or four years the rush was over, and except for a few places where there were some deep mines, the gold was gone and everyone had to find something else to do like farming or opening a store or looking for gold somewhere else.

"There is still gold around here," he said. "but there isn't very much of it. Some people still work small claims and there are even a few of them farther up on Gold Creek above the camp's property line. There are signs posted marking the boundaries of the claims and it is very wrong and against the law to try and get any gold from someone else's claim. In the old days that would get you shot or hung. Today you have to pay a fine. So be careful you don't jump somebody's claim if you ever try to pan for gold on your own!"

Worthy stood up and said, "Thank you Mr. Buchannan. Well, kids, what did you think of that? Did you have fun finding your gold?"

All the kids shouted out "Yes!"

"Gold," she said, "has always been valuable. In the Bible it is mentioned hundreds of times. The first place it is mentioned is in the Second Chapter of Genesis and that's about as early in the Bible as you can get!

"It was also an important part of the Jerusalem Temple. Israel honored God by giving the most precious things they had for God's use. The Temple was always a beautiful place for the people to worship and when they saw the golden Temple objects shining in the sun, they knew that God was being glorified.

"Gold was also one of the gifts brought to Jesus when he was born but the Bible doesn't tell us what happened to it.

"Later, Jesus taught there were things far more valuable than gold. 'Do not store up for yourselves treasures on earth, where moths and rust destroy, and where thieves break in and steal. But store up for yourselves treasures in heaven, where moths and rust do not destroy, and where thieves do not break in and steal. For where your treasure is, there your heart will be also.'

"So," Worthy asked, "Where is your treasure? Do you want to spend your whole life looking for gold?"

A few of the kids said "No!" but most just sat there waiting for her to go on.

"Even if you found a lot of gold," she continued, "you could spend it but when you died you couldn't take it with you, except to the grave.

"Jesus wants his followers to possess something so valuable that all the gold in the world wouldn't be able to pay for it. Jesus called this valuable thing the 'kingdom of Heaven.' For Jesus this kingdom was not a place but a way of life. He knew that gold could not make a person happy for very long and that gold does not make a person good or loving, either.

"When people love each other and take care of each other and treat each other with respect, and when people do this because God says it is the right way to live, then that is what the kingdom of Heaven is like.

"When we let Jesus into our hearts, we invite him to turn us into a person who can start living in that kingdom right away. Local churches should be places where people learn how to live this out with each other and Bible camps should be like that, too.

"Love is something that we get to keep when we join together with Jesus in eternal life. The gold we have to leave behind.

"So . . . tonight at the campfire you will be given a choice. You can choose to spend your whole life looking for your happiness in gold or you can spend your life looking for it in Jesus. The one will pass away. The other will last forever."

That is all that Worthy said that morning. When she was done, the kids split up and headed off with their cabin counselors.

LaShaun's group went down to the lake where Fil told each of them find a pinecone. Most of the pinecones they found were small ones. Glen was the only one to find a large, beat up cone from a Sugar Pine.

After they had gotten back in a circle Fil said, "Pinecones are where a pine tree's seeds are stored. If your pinecone had already opened up you can sometimes find a few seeds hiding down underneath the pointy parts. They are hard to find, though, because the seeds either fall out onto the ground or the squirrels, birds and chipmunks eat them."

Fil reached into his pocket and pulled out sealed baggie filled with what he said were pine nuts. He passed them around so everyone could see what they felt and tasted like.

"Have you noticed all the small pine trees sprouting up under the bigger trees around camp? They started out from a seed that fell out of a pinecone. That's how pine trees pass life on to the next generation of trees.

One of the boys said, "Ouch!" as he poked his finger onto one of the sharp thorns that protected the seeds inside his pinecone.

"When God created you," Fil continued, "he made a place in you where a seed with eternal life in it can grow. But this seed does not just start growing like the seeds in these pinecones. You see, there is one kind of pinecone that has seeds that won't grow unless the cone is burned up in a forest fire. If there isn't a fire then the seeds cannot grow.

"The seed of eternal life that God gives to us is like that. It cannot grow in us unless something else happens. What this seed needs is for us to live a perfect life. But the sad thing is that none of us are able to live a perfect life. The Sin that is in us will keep the seed from ever sprouting. Sin is like poison to the seed so, unless God does something about it, none of us will ever have that life come alive in us.

"The Good News is that Jesus came and lived the perfect life for us. Jesus did for us what we could never do for ourselves. Then, just like the pinecone has to die in the fire before its seed can grow, Jesus had to die on the cross before his seed of eternal life could begin to grow in us. This is what the Bible calls salvation.

"When we invite Jesus into our lives then that small seed starts growing. This is what the Bible calls being 'born again.'

"Jesus says that this seed starts out small but, if we help it along, it will grow larger and larger until our old life is taken over by the new one.

"Does any of this make any sense?"

Colin raised his hand first, "Yes, it does . . . at least for me. We all have to die. Just like a pine tree or a pinecone. And even the seed has to disappear so the new life can come out of it. I remember somewhere in the Bible it says that the old things go away and new ones come in their place. I think God gives us this new life so that when the old one dies, we still are alive . . .

alive forever. I think that's what you said. Did I get it right?"

Fil stood there thinking for a long time before he said, "Yes, Colin. I think you got it right. And this life comes from Jesus and from no one else. If you want, you can think of this as sort of a story; like the ones Jesus told to help his followers understand things better."

Fil asked the boys to bow their heads for prayer: "Lord Jesus, thank you for living and dying for us. You were perfect for us so that your seed of life could grow in us. Please Lord, plant the seed in us and make it grow so that when the old part of us dies, we will have your new life ready to replace it; so we can live in your kingdom forever. Amen."

When the prayer was over, he told everyone to go back to the cabin, put their gold away in a safe place and then wash up for lunch.

LaShaun tried to find a good place to hide his gold but, after a while, he remembered what Worthy said about worrying about gold all the time. Jesus had said there were lots of things were more valuable than gold so instead of hiding it, LaShaun just stuck it in his suitcase with his dirty socks.

Chapter Fifteen
Triumphs and Trials
Friday Afternoon

Since they would be checking out of the camp the next morning at 10:00 a.m. this would be their last lunch at the camp that summer. LaShaun couldn't believe the week had gone by so quickly. He didn't want to say good-bye to Fil or to Marcy and he wanted to spend as much time with them as he could before they all had to leave.

He looked for Marcy and found her standing right behind him in the Dining Hall, smiling at him as if she had just thought of something funny.

"Hi, Marcy," he said. "Let's have lunch together, okay?"

"Okay," she said. "I'd like that."

So, they went through the food line together and carried their sliced turkey with gravy, mashed potatoes and green beans back to a table. Instead of sitting across from each other they sat down side by side like they did on the log down at the beach the day before.

They talked about the gold they had panned. They talked about how hot it was. They talked about pinecones and then Marcy asked if anyone in LaShaun's cabin had told any good stories last night.

"Yes," he said, "But there was only one last night,"

"Was it a good one? What was it about?"

LaShaun couldn't decide whether it had been a good story or not. The story had been very strange. It had been told very well but he had promised he wouldn't tell anyone about Colin.

"It was a story about a kid whose hair started growing real fast and wouldn't stop. It was sort of creepy and it didn't have a happy ending. I guess it was good story. But I hope there aren't any more like it."

Marcy just nodded her head and said, "Have you told any more stories since, you know, the one you told me yesterday?"

LaShaun shook his head "No" but, of course, Marcy couldn't see him shake it because they were sitting so close to each other they couldn't turn their heads far enough to keep looking at each other for very long.

He started to say that he had been feeling there was another story forming somewhere inside of him and that he felt like a mother might feel when she had a baby growing that was waiting to come out; but he wasn't sure Marcy would understand and besides, what if there wasn't a story there after all?

So, he just said, "I'll let you know if I hear a good one before . . . uh . . . before tomorrow when . . ."

Marcy finished the sentence by saying, ". . . when we have to go home . . . ."

Then, as if the idea had just popped into her head she asked, "Do you do email? Maybe we could email each other when we get home? I do it all the time on my computer."

LaShaun didn't want Marcy to go away but the thought of writing back and forth to a girl seemed strange and made him feel uncomfortable. It was another one of those new feelings that he had been having all week.

She had asked a good question so he said, "You have your own computer? Wow! We only have one at my house. It's on the dining room table and I can only use it when my Dad's at home. He opened an email account for me but I've never used it. I don't really have a lot of friends anyway. And a lot of the kids have smart phones and text and I don't have one of those, either."

Marcy had a smart phone but she didn't say anything about it.

Instead she said, "Let's trade addresses, both kinds, and promise to write each other at least once when we get home."

The camp bell rang. Lunch was over and everyone had to clean their trays and get ready for their last day of electives. So LaShaun and Marcy got up and headed off to change into their swim suits.

There weren't any games in the pool that day but the lessons were fun. The teacher had roped off one swimming lane and worked with one kid one at a time while the others were told to swim laps and to see how long they could float or swim without touching their feet to the bottom or their hands to the side of the pool.

For some kids this was hard, but for Marcy and LaShaun it was easy. They still didn't swim very fast and LaShaun did the dog paddle some of the time. But they both felt they had learned a lot that week.

When LaShaun was alone with the teacher, he told her how he and Marcy really wanted to swim out to the diving platform down at the lake but they weren't sure they could do it because they didn't want to drown.

He was surprised when the teacher said, "Oh, I don't think you would have any trouble swimming out to the platform. But I know how it feels to do something like that for the first time. If you think it might help, I'll go down with you after class and I'll swim next to you so . . . well . . . in case . . . out to the platform with you."

LaShaun said that would be great! And he couldn't wait to tell Marcy. When he did, she thought it was great too! Maybe they would get to the platform after all!

And that's exactly what happened.

At the end of class, the teacher gave each swimmer a "Certificate of Completion." She explained that this didn't count as a Red Cross certification but, on the back of each certificate there were boxes that she had checked listing all the skills they had practiced and how well each swimmer had done.

Marcy's marks were a little better than LaShaun's but they both had high marks. And, at the bottom of LaShaun's certificate the teacher had written, "LaShaun was the most improved and most enthusiastic of all my students this week."

When they walked to the lake Marcy asked the teacher why she hadn't seen anyone swimming in the lake with a life jacket?

"Wouldn't that be a good way to learn how to swim?"

But the teacher said, "No." That was a bad way to learn because you never learned to float without it.

"Remember?" she asked. "Floating was the first thing you learned this week. Besides, the lifeguard doesn't want anyone out in the deep water who doesn't know how to swim without a life jacket. It just isn't safe."

At the lake the teacher asked, "Do you want to swim out all together or with me one at a time?"

Marcy said, "All at the same time" and LaShaun said, "One at a time."

They said it at the same time and they all laughed until LaShaun said, "You go first and then I'll go."

So LaShaun watched as Marcy got in the water and took a deep breath. She pushed herself towards the diving platform with her feet and started swimming as hard and as fast as she could.

He could hear their teacher saying, "Slow down, Marcy. You'll get all tired out. Take your time and relax. That's it . . . that's better . . ."

After what seemed only a minute or two, Marcy was climbing up the ladder and standing on the diving platform smiling and waving for LaShaun to join her.

The teacher swam back to the beach and she and LaShaun got into the water. LaShaun knew that he swam almost as well as Marcy so he knew he could do it.

186

He swam for a while and then stopped and treaded water to catch his breath for a moment before swimming the rest of the way without stopping again. He climbed up the ladder and felt as though he wanted to give Marcy a big hug. She felt the same way but, of course, they give each other a high-five instead.

The teacher had stayed in the water and, after they had finished celebrating, they went over and bent down to say "Thank you."

The teacher said, "You're welcome," and added, "I'm going back to change out of my swimsuit. You're both good swimmers and you don't need me to swim back to the beach. I enjoyed having you both in my class. I hope you can do a lot more swimming before the summer is over."

Marcy and LaShaun both looked at each other and smiled. And then they were alone on the diving platform with the big kids for the first time.

For a while they took turns jumping into the water and climbing back up on the ladder but after a while that got boring. So, they decided to lie down on their stomachs in the sun. When they felt their skin getting hot Marcy remembered that they hadn't put on any sunscreen since class and that maybe they shouldn't lie in the sun for so long.

They stood up on the platform and looked all around at the lake, the mountains, the trees and the camp buildings scattered along the shore and up the side of the hill. They looked at the willows where Gold Creek flowed into the lake and they looked up at the cross on the hill where they had seen the full beauty of the night sky.

Marcy said, "I'll race you back to the beach! Last one there is a rotten egg!"

But LaShaun reminded her what the teacher had said about taking their time and being relaxed when they swam. So, they jumped into the water and slowly swam and floated and paddled side by side all the way back to the shore.

As they swam, LaShaun found it hard to believe he had actually swum out to the diving platform and was already swimming back. He wondered if this experience was like gold: something that was exciting and fun for a while but didn't last forever.

Before he stepped out of the water, he had decided that it wasn't like gold at all. The swimming, and Fil and Marcy and the camp, were all worth a lot more than gold. He imagined himself in heaven and he didn't think that gold would matter much to him there. But these other things would be special to him forever.

When they got to shore, they dried off with their towels, got some hot chocolate and sat together on the log, watching the other kids swimming, splashing, diving and yelling in the water. This time they didn't talk and there were no stories to be told. At that moment they were the story. And neither of them wanted the story to end.

When the camp bell rang, they looked at each other and smiled and then ran back to their cabins. When LaShaun got to his cabin he saw the camp director, Worthy, the camp nurse and Ralph in a small circle talking with Fil. Fil wasn't saying anything but he was nodding his head up and down. He wasn't looking at anyone but was sort of looking down at his feet and then looking around as though he was very interested in studying the trees. He wasn't smiling, either.

Soon, they all put their hands on Fil's head and shoulders. Although he couldn't hear the words, LaShaun could tell that the camp director and Worthy were praying . . . praying for Fil. None of it looked normal and it didn't look as though it was a good thing for Fil or for anyone.

After the prayer, Fil went over towards the basketball court by himself and stood for a minute or two with his back to the cabin. Then he turned and walked back looking as though he was trying hard to smile. The director, Worthy and the nurse had left but Ralph was still there, looking very serious with his hands in his pockets looking back and forth between Fil and the Elijah boys who had all gathered together, in front of the cabin door.

Fil walked up and said, "Boys. I'm going to have to go. I don't want to but I have to go. They just . . . I just heard . . . my mother was in a car accident this morning in Stockton and was hurt . . . hurt really bad. I don't know if . . .well, I have to go."

Several of the boys started to get tears in their eyes and none of them knew what to say. LaShaun felt as though there was suddenly a big hole where his stomach had been.

Fil had told him how his father had died like in the story LaShaun had told. He remembered that in his story, the boy's mother died, too. Is that what was happening? Was his story still coming true?

Fil walked into the cabin and started packing up his things.

"I'm going to miss you," he said to no one in particular. "I didn't want the summer to end like this.

"You all know Ralph? He's going to be your counselor for what's left of the week. Be nice to him . . . like you have all been to me.

"Now . . . well, I've got to go."

He started to walk out the door but after a few steps he stopped, turned back and said, "I want to pray before I go."

So, the boys gathered in front of him. He looked each one in the eye and said their name, and then he bowed his head.

"Heavenly Father," he said, "All good things come from you and this week has been one of those good things. Each of these boys has been a good thing for me too, and I thank you for each one of them. Now there's something bad happening and I don't know what good can come out of it but I know you can and . . ."

Fil stopped in mid-sentence and LaShaun thought that it was like the prayer Fil had given when they first met him, when he had forgotten what he was going to say and just stopped in the middle of it . . . except this time Fil looked as though he was about to cry.

LaShaun, without any advance warning, found himself walking up to Fil. He put his hand on his shoulder, like they had done with Colin the night before.

Some of the other boys did the same and he heard himself saying, "God, I know that you will bring something good out of this for Fil because you love him just like we do, and like his mother does, and like his father did and . . .and . . . ."

LaShaun found himself starting to say, " . . . and that it will be a fun week for all of us," but he caught himself just in time, took a deep breath and just said, "Amen."

Fil said, "Thanks, you guys. Remember, no matter what happens to me or my Mom or to any of you, remember that God is bigger, stronger, smarter, greater, and . . . and . . . more full of love than anything else in the world. And remember that God . . . ."

He stopped for a moment before starting over.

"Boys, just remember the stories; the stories we've told each other; the stories we've heard from the Bible; the stories some of us have written in our journals and the stories we have been creating all week during our time here at camp. Maybe all of it together will be the best story of all; the one you take back home and tell to your Mom or your Dad. But be sure to include God and Jesus in your story, because . . . well . . . I guess that's all. Now I really have to go. Bye!"

He waved a little wave and turned to walk back towards the parking lot and his car.

Ralph started to say something but LaShaun ran into the cabin and rummaged around in his suitcase for something. When he found what he was looking for he stuck it in his pocket and ran after Fil. He caught up with him just past the Dining Hall.

"Fil!" he yelled.

Fil stopped and turned around.

"LaShaun," he said, "I really need to go . . . ."

But LaShaun reached into his pocket and put something into Fil's hand.

When Fil looked at it, he saw a small, smooth stone about the size of a thimble. It was bluish-black in color with small veins of reddish-orange running through it. He held the stone in his hand and slowly began to rub it gently between his thumb and index finger. The stone began to grow warm and, in his imagination, it began to glow.

He looked up at LaShaun and said, "Thank you for everything. I think I'm going to miss you more than anything. God has his hand on you, LaShaun, and I know that God has some wonderful plans for you. I don't know what they are going to be but I know that your life, like a good story, still has lots of pages in it. Like in a book, you won't know what's going to happen next until you turn the pages one by one. If you let Jesus into your life, your life's story will be joined with his. And if you join your story with his, then you already know that your story will have a happy ending; no matter what might happen between now and then."

He paused and added, "I know that no matter what happens to my Mom, her story and mine will both have happy endings, too . . . because of Jesus."

He started to turn but paused and looked back down at his hand.

Then he looked back up at LaShaun and said, "Thank you for this. I promise I will never, ever, throw it away."

He gave LaShaun a small, strained smile and then turned, walked away and was gone.

LaShaun stood there, feeling as if the world had just gotten smaller; as if a part of it had disappeared into space.

He looked around, and the trees looked the same and the camp looked the same. But he had the same feeling he experienced when he was with Marcy at the beach the day before. The world was the same but different, and he was the same but different, too.

He felt like a lump of clay that someone kept squeezing into new shapes or like the piece of construction paper he had cut up to make his Coat of Arms.

If he had carried these thoughts a little farther, he would have wondered if he was being shaped into something beautiful or being cut up and used before being thrown away. These were some of the feelings and thoughts that were bumping and scraping against each other in his heart.

Once again, he felt like a juggler, trying to keep too many rocks in the air at the same time. This time, as he stood there just past the Dining Hall by himself, he bowed his head and asked Jesus to help him with the juggling.

When he got back to the cabin, he saw that Ralph had somehow gotten a small bucket full of raw eggs. He had paired the boys up and had them standing face to face with each other. Because LaShaun was missing, Ralph had to partner-up with Phil to make the teams come out even.

He gave every pair of boys an egg and asked one of them to pass it over to his partner. Then he had everyone take a step backwards and pass the egg to the other partner again.

As the boys got farther and farther apart, they had to toss the eggs farther and farther.

Soon Phil dropped Ralph's egg and then Robert's egg broke all over Marty's hand. That left Colin and Garret, and Mo and Glen as the only teams left.

On the next throw, Mo's egg sailed six feet over Glen's head and Garret's egg went straight up in the air and came down so fast that Colin jumped out of the way, as it hit the ground with a "splat!"

The boys were laughing and having a good time until they saw LaShaun standing there and remembered what had just happened.

LaShaun wanted to be laughing, too, so he said, "Hey, that looks like fun. I'm sorry I missed out. I've got an idea. At our church picnic each year we have a shoe kick."

The other boys and Ralph looked puzzled.

"What we do is we all line up side by side and loosen one of our shoes. Then we take turns to see who can kick their shoe the farthest."

Everyone thought that sounded like fun so they all lined up and started kicking.

The smaller boys went first. Garret's shoe caught on his foot and only went a few feet but Colin's went almost to the cabin. Phil's went even further but Mo's went up high and came down short and LaShaun's did the same.

Then the three bigger boys took their turns, confident that they would win easily. But Robert's shoe came off late and sailed backwards over his head into the trees. Marty's shoe landed on the cabin roof but not quite as far as Phil's.

Only Glen was left. He stepped back and made a running start and when he got to the line, he threw his foot into the air and fell over backwards onto the ground. His shoe stayed on his foot the whole time until, when he hit the ground, it fell off his upraised leg and landed on his forehead.

Everyone laughed so hard that even Glen joined in.

Phil won the shoe kick contest but nobody really noticed or cared because of what had happened to Glen. Ralph found a long pole and managed to knock Marty's shoe off of the cabin roof and then they all stood staring at each other wondering what to do next.

Mo said, "I know what we need to do. We never finished putting the glue on the back of our family crests."

Everyone said that was a good idea, so Marty and Robert found Fil's craft bag and the tray with the crests on it, and in a few minutes, everyone was done with the gluing. They all noticed how clear the glue had dried on the front side and LaShaun thought his had turned out well.

When they had cleaned up Ralph looked at his watch and said, "It's a little early but why don't we just have free play until dinner. I'll see you at the campfire."

And the boys scattered in all directions.

LaShaun didn't know what to do so he wandered across the camp past the Dining Hall, past the parking area and the Director's House and over to the girl's cabins. He saw Marcy's group finishing up their craft time. They had cut out snowflakes on folded pieces of paper and then used the patterns as stencils to make colorful designs on pastel-colored scarves. Most of the scarves looked all smudged up but some of them had turned out beautifully. Marcy wasn't happy with hers and wouldn't even let LaShaun see it.

When their group time was over Marcy put her scarf away in the cabin, got her jacket and started walking towards the Dining Hall with LaShaun. Tracy had told them that Fil had left because his mother had been in an accident so Marcy already knew LaShaun would be worried and upset. She wasn't surprised when he took her hand and led her past the Dining Hall and up the side of the hill. Soon they were above the boy's cabins and, a few steps further on, they came to Gold Creek. Just above them was a clump of Manzanita bushes and, on the other side of the bushes, was the secret place that only Fil had known about.

They stopped holding hands and, without saying anything, they sat down at one of the tables facing each other.

Marcy finally broke the silence by asking, "Are you all okay? I heard about Fil. Is he all right?"

"He'll be all right, I think," LaShaun said. "He told me that if we are with Jesus then our stories will always have happy endings. I've been thinking about it and I'm not sure that some of the stories that Fil told us at night had happy endings."

Marcy interrupted by asking, "But did those stories have Jesus in them?"

And it didn't take LaShaun long to answer, "No, I guess they didn't."

"Well then," Marcy said, "maybe that's why they didn't have happy endings."

LaShaun had been thinking about stories all week and he remembered what Marcy had said about God telling all the best stories. As far as he could remember, every story in the Bible that God told about Jesus had a happy ending. Being betrayed by Judas and dying on the cross weren't happy parts of the story but they weren't the end of the story, either. The end of the story was Easter when Jesus was alive again.

When it came to Jesus, even when a story seemed to have a sad ending, like with Colin and his cancer, Easter was nearby, waiting around the corner like one of the kids hiding behind a tree; just waiting to pop out and catch someone by surprise; but with good news instead of a "Boo!"

He looked at Marcy and said, "I wonder if my story and my Dad's story will have happy endings?"

Marcy wasn't sure what he meant because LaShaun had never talked about his family to her before. But he kept on talking so she kept listening.

"I'm not sure about my mother, though. She's in prison. Did I tell you that?"

Marcy shook her head, "No."

"Well," said LaShaun, "she is. And I don't know if she'll ever get out. And I'm not sure if there will be a happy ending for any of us or all of us. I just don't know."

And Marcy and LaShaun just sat there, looking across the table at each other wondering what to say next.

Among the other things that had been on his mind all day was the question that Robert and Marty had asked him at breakfast that morning. Was he going to come forward at tonight's campfire and let Jesus into his heart as Lord and Savior or not? He thought that he now knew what he was going to do but, since Fil was gone, he wanted to ask Marcy about it.

"Marcy?" he asked. "Are you going to go forward at the campfire tonight? I mean when they ask us to make a decision about Jesus?"

Marcy answered by saying, "I went forward at the camp I went to earlier this summer so I wasn't sure whether I needed to do it again. I guess it wouldn't hurt anything if I did."

She waited for LaShaun to say something but he didn't.

So she said, "If I go down will you go with me? I'll do it if you will. We could go down together."

Chapter Sixteen
I've Been Set Free
Friday Evening

They talked for so long that they missed dinner, but when they heard the camp bell ring they walked down the hill to the campfire and sat together on the same bench that had been so hot when LaShaun had sat on it the previous Sunday.

Back then, he had felt sad and alone. He didn't know anybody and he had decided that he didn't want to be at camp at all. The air was too hot, the cabin was too stuffy and Fil had seemed to be too much of an idiot.

But so much had changed in just a few short days. As he looked around, the camp really did look exactly as it had when he had first arrived. But he had changed in ways he still did not understand. In some way's life had gotten more complicated for him but, for some reason, it seemed as if he was juggling everything much better than before. Maybe he had already made up his mind about Jesus. Maybe Jesus had already become a part of his story and maybe he had become a part of Jesus' story, too. Maybe tonight would simply be a chance to stand up and announce it to everyone else.

Worthy led the singing and then two of the kitchen staff performed a skit about making up their minds about something. When they had finished, Worthy opened up her Bible and read from Matthew 11:28-29.

"Jesus said, 'Come to me, all you who are weary and burdened, and I will give you rest. Take my yoke upon you and learn from me, for I am gentle and humble in heart, and you will find rest for your souls.'

"Remember," Worthy asked, "the story about Jesus knocking at the door of your heart? Where he hopes you will let him in to live with you?

"Tonight's an opportunity for you to come to Jesus and to let him come to you. Maybe you're hurting or maybe you're afraid of something. Maybe you feel weary and burdened. Maybe you are worried about life and death or maybe you feel bad about being a failure because you aren't able to be perfect.

"Jesus says, 'Come to me . . . and I will give you rest.'

"He is the Lord of the universe but he wants you to make him the Lord of your life. He is the Savior of the world but he wants you to claim him as the Savior of your life as well.

"Jesus doesn't force any of this on you. But he does touch you with his Holy Spirit to encourage you to say 'Yes' to him.

"If you feel that Jesus is calling to you tonight, I hope and pray that you will say 'Yes.'

"On Jesus' behalf I invite you right now, to come to him in faith and in hope, to welcome him into your life as your Lord and Savior."

Worthy stood still, waiting as the other two counselors played guitars. They were joined by other camp staff in singing softly:

"I have decided to follow Jesus, no turning back, no turning back."

And then they sang,

"Just as I am without one plea but that your life was shed for me . . . O Lamb of God, I come . . . I come."

And, at the end, they sang the version of *Amazing Grace* by Chris Tomlin that goes,

Amazing grace, how sweet the sound
  that saved a wretch like me;
I once was lost, but now I'm found,
  was blind, but now I see.
My chains are gone I've been set free,
  my God, my Savior has ransomed me.
And like a flood His mercy rains,
  Unending love, Amazing grace.
The earth shall soon dissolve like snow,
  the sun forbear to shine
But God, Who called me here below,
  will be forever mine."

As it turned out, every boy in the Elijah cabin came forward that night. Maybe it had something to do with Fil, maybe it had something to do with Colin and his cancer, maybe it had something to do with the stories and maybe it had something to do with the Holy Spirit reshaping their hearts and minds through all of these things during the week.

Marcy and LaShaun came forward when they heard the words, "My chains are gone, I've been set free." They didn't hold hands but their hearts were joined together in a way that only the best of friends could ever understand. They stood with the light of the campfire on their faces, the wood smoke in their noses and the popping and crackling of the sparks in their ears. When Worthy prayed, they bowed their heads as she said,

"Lord Jesus, take these as your children and as your disciples. Cover them with your love, your forgiveness and your salvation. Fill them with your Holy Spirit so they will be faithful to you all the days of their lives. I thank you and praise you for what you have done for them. And we promise this day, each in our own way, that we will do all that we can to love one another as you have loved us. I pray this in your holy name. Amen."

When the prayer was over, some of the counselors went around and gave small booklets to everyone who had come forward. They also encouraged each of them to join a local church and, if they had not been baptized before, to be baptized into their new faith as a follower of Jesus.

After everyone had gone back to their seat Worthy shared some information about the next day's breakfast, clean up and check out. She thanked everyone for making this the best week ever. Then the camp director came forward and said "Thank you." He gave a closing blessing and the campfire was over.

LaShaun thought that he would feel different but he didn't. Maybe it was because the "different" feeling had already happened to him earlier. But he was happy. Everything was perfect except that Fil wasn't there to share it with. LaShaun knew how happy Fil would be to know that everyone in his group had come forward that night.

When it came time to go back to their cabins LaShaun took Marcy's right hand in his left hand and stood facing her. Marcy reached out her other hand and they stood quietly, looking at each other, thinking their own thoughts and, perhaps, dreaming their own dreams. When the moment came, they dropped their hands and embraced in a hug that lasted, perhaps, a little longer than either of them felt comfortable with. When it was over, LaShaun felt both happier and sadder than he had ever felt before. It was a feeling he treasured and one he never forgot for the rest of his life.

LaShaun walked back to his cabin without Fil and without Marcy, but . . . and he felt very sure of this . . . he walked back to the cabin with Jesus.

Once everyone was in the cabin Ralph asked what they usually did before they went to bed.

Mo said, "We write in our journals and then, when the lights are turned off, we tell stories. Do you tell stories?"

Ralph said, "No, I'm not very good at telling stories but someone else can tell one if they want."

Everyone in the room looked at LaShaun and LaShaun was wondering if tonight was when the story was going to pop out of him like a newborn baby.

"Let me think about it," he said.

Then everyone began writing in their journal about the day's events. Every boy in the cabin wrote down the ways they had seen God that day and they wrote and wrote for thirty minutes before the first boy put his pencil down.

Ralph was amazed, for he had never seen boys this age act like this before.

When the last boy had finished writing, Mo spoke.

"Well, it's time for lights out and time for a story."

Marty called out, "Ralph, when we get to zero, turn out the lights."

And all the boys started counting, "Ten . . . nine . . . eight . . . and when they came to zero the room went dark and there was silence.

"Well?" someone in the room asked.

And then another voice said, "Well?"

And then another and another until someone said, "LaShaun" and then everyone was saying "LaShaun" over and over.

They all did this quietly because they didn't want Worthy to come over to see if they were killing a fatted calf.

They all stopped chanting when Garret said, "Shhh," and then there was silence again.

The silence ended almost as soon as it began when the boys heard LaShaun say, "I have a story."

While the boys had been chanting, LaShaun had actually felt pain in his body as he tried to work his story out into the open.

When Garret said, "Shhh," the struggle ended and he was at peace, knowing the time had come for the story to be born.

"There was a boy," he began. "He was young, he was invincible and, as far as he could tell, he was immortal. He felt as though he could run forever and not get tired. He could walk for miles and miles and even climb mountains without missing a single step. He felt as if he could soar like an eagle. His hair was black, the grass was green and the flowers were in bloom.

"Evening came and he climbed into bed and fell asleep, dreaming of tomorrow.

"When he awoke, he found himself in a strange room filled with strange smells and strange sounds. He tried to get out of his bed but he couldn't even roll over. He hurt all over and didn't feel well at all.

"Soon a man wearing a white coat came in and lifted him out of his bed and into a chair. He needed to go to the bathroom but there was a bag and he used it from where he sat. There was a window in his room and he could see that it was winter. The grass was brown and there were no flowers to be seen.

"There was also a mirror in the room that went all the way down to the floor. In the mirror he saw an old man with hair that was thin and white with streaks of gray. His skin was all wrinkled and the chair he sat in had wheels. One side of the man's face seemed to sag and, when he called out to the man in the white coat for help, he heard a strange and frightening moan come out of his mouth.

Then the man remembered that he was no longer a boy and that the man in the mirror was himself. And he wept.

"As the day moved on the man sat and sat as if he was a statue. He imagined what it would be like if he were left outside. He imagined that the birds would sit on his head and leave droppings on him as they flew away.

"The monotony was unbroken except for the endless droning of the television in his room. When food came, it was fed to him with a spoon. It tasted like sawdust or like dry, un-moistened oatmeal and made him gag. The man in the white coat held up a plastic cup with a straw for him to suck the water into his mouth.

"There was nothing for him to do except to think and to remember the past. The future held no interest for him at all, for he did not know any stories about the future. But, ah, the stories he knew of the past! They were the only things he owned that were of any value. And he knew so many of them.

"There were stories of his childhood; of loving parents and a brother and a sister. There were stories of bee stings and cuts and scrapes from rolling down hills and falling off of bicycles. There were stories of school where the names of teachers and friends were long forgotten. There were stories of work well done, of songs sung, of music played and of poems filled with passion and written with a pen of fire. There was the story of a girl, a story that was like a treasure to him. And there were the stories of his wife and his children; and it was those stories that he loved to tell more than any of the others.

"There were sad stories, too; stories of family and friends who once were but were no more, except in his memory where they still lived lives as real as his own.

"The stories brought comfort to the man. But stories are not only for remembering, but for sharing. Sadly, the man could no longer tell his stories and, so far as he could tell, there was no key that could unlock the vault in which they were kept.

"Because of these things, the man grieved and wished that he would die.

"The saddest thing of all was that the man did not know he had one final story to tell. It was a story that could be shared without being spoken; a story that could touch the heart of others and bring them sorrow and joy, laughter and tears. It was a good story; a beautiful story and it had taken him a lifetime before he was ready to tell it.

"He did not know it but every day he was telling that story and offering it as a gift to anyone who had ears to hear and eyes to see. But for the longest time there was no one who took the time to listen and no one who took the time to look.

"One day a boy poked his head through the door to his room. He was a boy who had come with his mother to visit someone in another room; a person he did not know and did not care to know. The boy preferred to choose his own friends and so he poked his head through the door to see if there might be a friend on the other side.

"What the boy heard and what he saw in that room was a story. It was a story of a man. It was a story filled with adventure, mystery and romance. It was a story told by the lines etched in the skin and seen in the gnarled knuckles of a hand. It was a story that no one but the boy was able or willing to see or

211

hear. And it was a story that captured the boy's heart; a story that embraced him with a fierce and gentle love.

"The boy and his mother came often and, as the mother sat with her friend, the boy sat with his. Every day the man told his story and the boy listened. It was not long before the boy began to tell stories of his own. He told stories that only boys could tell. There were stories of running and leaping; of long walks and of hills and mountains to be climbed. Like all good stories his stories had the power to break down walls and to unlock vaults. The story of the boy joined with the story of the man and the stories became one.

"So it was that the man found himself running and leaping again without growing weary. He took long walks and climbed high mountains without ever missing a step, and, joined as one with the boy, he found himself flying like an eagle.

"Spring had returned to the world and through his window he could see green grass and beautiful flowers. In the mirror, however, he still saw an old man sitting in a chair. But in the face of the man he saw the eyes of a boy; eyes that twinkled with mischief and gazed longingly at worlds far beyond the farthest horizon. Beyond that horizon he saw the future, and, for the first time in many, many years, he saw that the future still had a story to tell. His soul was filled with wonder, with joy, and with peace.

"In that future there were family and friends yet to come. There were sad stories and stories filled with laughter. There was music, too, and singing, and poetry. And there was the boy. There was always the boy.

"The day came when the story the man had to tell came to an end and the boy felt a great sadness. But the sadness became a story of its own and the man's story was joined with the sadness and redeemed it.

"It came to pass that the story of the man and the story of the boy soared to the heavens and become joined with the story of angels, whose story was the story of God. It was a story that told of a cross and of an empty tomb; a story that told of death and of life; a story that told of a time when old men and boys would be one and the same; a story that had no beginning and no ending; a story that would go on forever."

LaShaun had nothing more to say and, as the boys slept, their hair became gray. But their eyes twinkled with mischief.

Chapter Seventeen
A New Story Begins
Saturday Morning

The next morning there were no devotions in the Elijah cabin but LaShaun wrote in his journal anyway. He wrote that he had seen God in the story he had told the night before. But he also wrote that the story was beyond his understanding.

Then he added, "If God ever wants me to understand it, I will understand it."

The boys packed their things before breakfast. Few words were spoken, for everything that needed to be said had already been said.

Breakfast was scrambled eggs and bacon and, for the first time that week, all the boys from the Elijah cabin sat together at the same table. No one could say exactly why they felt so close to each other but they did.

After breakfast, all the kids in camp carried their suitcases, duffle bags, sleeping bags and pillows down to the parking lot where they waited to be picked up, signed out, and driven away.

Marcy and LaShaun piled their stuff next to each other, sat on the ground and waited to be separated from each other, probably forever.

As they sat, LaShaun took the coat of arms he had made and gave it as a gift to Marcy. He pointed out which star was his and which star was hers.

Marcy then reached into her suitcase and handed LaShaun the box she had made with the Bible verse that had reminded her of LaShaun's story. As they exchanged gifts neither of them spoke; for there was no need for words.

It seemed impossible to LaShaun that this could be happening. But with God, he knew, nothing was impossible . . . even, apparently, moments like this. So, he and Marcy sat and waited for the end to come.

It was not long before Marcy's grandparents pulled up in their SUV.

Marcy introduced them to LaShaun and LaShaun said, "Nice to meet you," and they said, "What a polite young man you are."

They hugged Marcy and said that they wanted to hear all about her week at camp on the drive back to their house.

Before she got into the car, Marcy walked over to LaShaun, and for the second time that week, she kissed him on the cheek.

LaShaun blushed but Marcy just smiled and said, "LaShaun, thank you for being my friend this week. Thank you for your story, and . . . send me an email, okay?"

LaShaun just nodded his head.

But before Marcy turned to leave, he took her hand in his and said, "Thank you . . . it was fun."

It wasn't much of a "good-bye" but it was enough, and Marcy knew what he meant by it.

After that, there was one more smile, one wave good-bye and then there was nothing left for LaShaun to do except sit down and wait for his father.

When his father drove up, he gave LaShaun a handshake, a hug, and a kiss on his forehead. LaShaun couldn't remember the last time his father had kissed him. But without even thinking about it he knew that the kiss was his father's way of saying that he had missed him.

And that made LaShaun feel like he was ready to go home.

His father signed him out, tossed LaShaun's gear in the back seat, made sure LaShaun was buckled into his seatbelt, started the engine, and drove away towards home.

LaShaun did not wave good-bye to anyone and did not even feel the need to turn around for one final look at the camp. He sensed that a new story was beginning to take shape somewhere deep inside of him. He didn't know what it would be, but he knew that the stories of Fil and Marcy, the Elijah boys, the swimming platform and his coming forward at the campfire would be a part of the new one.

He couldn't wait to hear it!

OTHER BOOKS BY JAMES A. TWEEDIE

Long Beach Short Stories

Cycles

BOOKS IN THE MIKE MAURISON SERIES

Book 1
I Want My MoMA
A Year in the Life of Mike Maurison, Private Eye

Book 2
To Have and To Hold
A Month in the Life of Mike Maurison, Private Eye

Book 3
Treasure Hunt
A Week in the Life of Mike Maurison, Private Eye

Book 4
Smoke and Mirrors
A Day in the Life of Mike Maurison, Private Eye

All books are published by Dunecrest Press and are
available on Amazon.com as paperback or Kindle

Made in the USA
Monee, IL
12 July 2020

35602752R00125